Praise for

"Should give kids **plenty to think about.**"
—*Kirkus Reviews*

"[Zephaniah] does an **excellent** job of
animating his setting."   —*Booklist*

"Zephaniah paints **a sympathetic portrait**
of Martin Turner, a burn victim, who changes as
much on the inside as on the outside after a car
accident leaves his face severely disfigured....
Martin himself is believable enough to be
appealing. Kids will tune in to this book's
clear message about appearances."
—*Publishers Weekly*

face

BENJAMIN ZEPHANIAH

BLOOMSBURY

Dedicated to all the staff and supporters of
Changing Faces. A great bunch of dudes working
to raise awareness and increase the resources
devoted to the care and rehabilitation of
facially disfigured people.

Changing Faces, 1 & 2 Junction Mews, London W2 1PN
U.K. Registered Charity No: 1011222

www.benjaminzephaniah.com

Copyright © 1999 by Benjamin Zephaniah
First published in Great Britain 1999
First published in the United States 2002
This edition published 2004

Published by Bloomsbury Publishing, New York and London
Distributed to the trade by Holtzbrinck Publishers

Library of Congress Cataloging-in-Publication Data
Zephaniah, Benjamin.
Face / by Benjamin Zephaniah.
p. cm.
Summary: A teenage boy's face is disfigured in an automobile accident,
and he must learn to deal with the changes in his life.
ISBN 1-58234-774-3 (hardcover)
ISBN 1-58234-921-5 (paperback)
[1. Disfigured persons—Fiction. 2. Traffic accidents—Fiction.
3. Prejudices—Fiction. 4. England—Fiction.] I. Title.
PZ7.Z426 Fac 2002
[Fic]—dc21
2002022758

Printed in the United States of America by Quebecor World Fairfield
7 9 10 8 6

Bloomsbury Publishing, Children's Books, U.S.A.
175 Fifth Avenue
New York, New York 10010

All papers used by Bloomsbury Publishing are natural, recyclable products
made from wood grown in well-managed forests. The manufacturing processes
conform to the environmental regulations of the country of origin.

MARTIN

I always thought that these things happened to other people until it happened to me. The experience really changed my life, but I found out who my friends were and I got to know me.

NATALIE

I hate people who discriminate. I think we're all equal. But I have ambition, I want to make it big and, let's face it, I'm trying to sell an image. It's nothing personal.

MATTHEW

I'm no angel, I just try to keep out of trouble. It's OK to have a bit of fun but I know that if you play with fire you get burnt. That's reality.

MARK

I was lucky, it's as simple as that. I can't keep looking back and feeling guilty. I'm not going to go around blaming anyone or moaning. I'm just looking after number one.

DR OWENS

The priority in post-burn treatment is firstly to create a 100 percent skin cover and secondly, to rectify any major facial or other abnormalities. Facial reconstruction is my area of expertise. I've worked on many faces in my time and I can tell you that the characteristics of a person's face have nothing to do with their intelligence or their loveability.

CHAPTER 1

~ The Gang of Three ~

The last minutes of the last lesson of the last day of term were ticking away, and Martin Turner could not wait to be set free. The minutes dragged on as Mr Lincoln, the form tutor, lectured the class on using holiday time constructively, not giving the school a bad name and staying safe.

'Remember all that we talked about in Drug Awareness Week,' he said. 'And don't go giving your parents a nervous breakdown.'

Martin raised his hand to get the teacher's attention. He had his 'up to no good' look on his face and everyone in the class knew it. 'Sir, have you got any advice on holiday sex?'

The whole class burst into uncontrollable laughter as Martin stood up, turned and bowed to the class like an actor takes a bow at the theatre.

'QUIET,' Mr Lincoln shouted at the top of his voice. 'Sit down, Turner, and take that grin off your face.'

Mr Lincoln surveyed the class as if it were his domain. 'While you are out there having fun, take time to consider the fact that next term will be your last in this year,' he said. 'So now you should seriously begin to consider what type of employment or further education you will be seeking. I suggest that you don't waste this holiday period. Talk to your parents, read up on your options and remember there is no reason why you can't use some of the time for study.'

'STUDY!' came a cry from someone at the back.

'Yes, study.'

Now it was Matthew's turn. 'Sir, I thought that holidays were for holidays? If we have to think about work and school stuff in the holidays, then it's not a holiday, is it?'

'That's right,' Mark added. 'Holidays are not for working, holidays are for not working.'

'Education never ceases,' Mr Lincoln replied as the electronic bell rang out all around the school. There were no 'goodbye sirs', just a mad rush for everyone to grab their belongings and escape as if there were some emergency. Even Mr Lincoln seemed relieved that school was over for a while. But as each member of his class raced past him, he looked lonely and neglected, slowly packing his books into his old leather briefcase.

Outside the school, crowds gathered. Meetings, raves and parties were planned. Pupils split into their various groups and gangs. Sometimes at the end of the school day, fights would happen, but not today – today it was all cool. Even the Big Six Posse, the most respected and feared school gang in the whole of East Ham, were celebrating, practising dance moves and wishing 'peace an luv' to everyone in sight.

One of Martin's best friends was Mark Thorpe, but in school Mr Lincoln insisted that Martin sat in the front row and Mark at the back. Even so, they still managed to cause trouble and entertain the class. In other lessons they would be in the same class as Matthew, who was the laid back third member of the gang. They called themselves the Gang of Three. Together you could feel them planning the defeat of order.

In truth the Gang of Three was just a name they called themselves; to others they were simply known as Martin Turner and his mates – Matthew the quiet one and Mark the silly one. But the three did have a reputation for mischief making and playing tricks. Almost every page of Martin's school reports said that he could do better but that he needed to pay more attention. Martin saw school as somewhere he went because he had to by law, so the least he could do while he was there was to have some fun. Although he was one of the best gymnasts in school, he never made the team because he 'lacked discipline'.

The three also had a reputation for chasing girls.

Mark and Matthew were free and single and Martin was going out with Natalie Hepburn. But that didn't stop the three of them from admiring the scenery. What they called the scenery were the cars and the girls. Fast cars or cars that sounded fast were greeted with a collective 'Corrr' and girls were greeted with 'Hey', 'Look at her,' 'Come 'ere' and the occasional whistle. Mark and Matthew never found a girlfriend this way but they still insisted on using this tactic. On this particular afternoon Mark's eye was caught by Jennifer Hamilton from Year 11. She was sixteen years old, and a lot taller than him.

Mark whistled to her and shouted so that everyone could hear, 'Come 'ere, Jenny baby, and give us a kiss goodbye.'

She walked straight up to him, looked down on him and said, 'I'm here, boy, let's do it.'

Mark was shocked.

'OK, you start it,' he spluttered.

'What, do you want me to start without you?'

Laughter burst out as spectators gathered around, all wanting to see the action. Jennifer stood towering above Mark like a gladiator. Mark got himself into more trouble every time he spoke.

'I tell ya what, close yu eyes and I'll start.'

'Close my eyes. What's the matter, boy? Don't you want me to see you? Look, everyone else is watching, I wanna see too!'

The laughter got louder and now the crowd, girls and boys, started to shout encouragement.

'Do it, man, and do it good.'

'Teach him a lesson, girl!'

'Come on, Mark . . . show us how it's done.'

'Give her one for me.'

Even Jennifer cracked a smile when one of her best friends shouted, 'Don't hurt him, have mercy upon his lips, for he is young and fragile.'

'All right.' Mark got serious. 'Bend down and let's do the business.'

As Jennifer bent down towards him, Mark squeezed his eyes shut, every muscle on his face tensed and his feet gripping the floor. Jennifer put her hand under his chin and tilted his face towards the sky, the crowd sounding like supporters at a boxing match. Jennifer stuck out her tongue and unleashed it all over Mark's forehead.

The crowd roared with laughter. Mark opened his eyes and shouted, 'I'll kill you, Jennifer Ham!' Jennifer ran off laughing and Mark tried to give chase. As they ran around the playground it was easy to see that Mark was no match for her ability to dodge or her speed. She was six foot tall. He would take a multitude of steps for one of her gigantic strides.

That was the kind of thing that made Mark funny. He was desperate to try and be like Martin. He loved

11

Martin's confidence and sense of trickery but most of his tricks would backfire leaving him with egg (or saliva) on his face. Deep down he was a little unhappy about this.

Matthew was quite different. He liked a laugh but he was more cautious than the other two. Matthew could often be heard saying, 'What if we get caught?' or 'I don't know if this is a good idea,' when the other two were in full swing. When the gang were up to mischief, Martin and Mark always complained that Matthew slowed them down. He was continually doing good deeds. Once when they were being chased by the park keeper for doing high jumps over the tennis nets, Matthew actually stopped to return an old man's hat that had blown off his head and was drifting in the wind. The other two stuck by him because he did like a bit of fun – and anyway, they had been The Gang of Three since primary school days.

Some people thought of Natalie Hepburn as the fourth member of the gang – but she didn't. Natalie was her own person, an individual who just happened to be going out with this kid who thought he was a clever dick. Many of the girls in school had a lot of respect for Natalie because she would not allow anyone to push her around. She was a bit of a judo expert and she had once been used in a hair commercial because of her Mediterranean looks and her long black hair. She had been going out with Martin for five months now, which was the longest Martin had been out with anyone. Natalie loved Martin's looks – his brown eyes, his long, thick brown hair, which just rested on his shoulders, and his slim build. She knew that because Martin had such a cute baby face, lots of other girls found him good-looking. He had the kind of face many actors and impressionists would dream of, able to mimic almost any person or animal and able to convey any emotion in a second. Natalie knew that he was aware of this gift and always used it to his advantage, but she also knew that looks weren't everything. Her friends thought she was a bit mad for going out with him, but she reckoned there was an intelligent person under all that front and that maybe one day she would get to him.

Natalie knew just how to deal with Martin when he tried to see how far he could go. Just five months ago Pat James, who was in Year 9, really fancied Martin. Martin played it dangerously by sweet-talking both of them at the same time. When Natalie heard about this, she arranged for both of them to confront him together. Martin couldn't believe it. One dinner time they walked up to him in the playground and demanded that he decide who he really liked. He chose Natalie of course and Pat James had hated the two of them ever since. But Natalie didn't leave it at that. Once Pat was out of the way, she made Martin ask for forgiveness in front of all her friends and demanded that he bought her a friendship ring costing no less than ten pounds. That was Natalie's way.

CHAPTER 2

~ The Eastenders ~

The first few days of the holidays passed slowly. It rained a lot and the Gang of Three's greatest pleasure was sleeping late. By the second week the sun had begun to shine, so Martin, Mark and Matthew started looking for action. On some days this meant going over to Wanstead Flats, grassland on the edge of Epping Forest where girls walked and where football was played. It was like a park with the attitude of a beach.

Martin loved the forest. He thought other areas of the East End were concrete jungles, with no space to breathe. The Flats were a quick escape to greenery. He knew the area well but he took much of its cultural diversity for granted. At school he learnt how in the sixteenth century French Protestant refugees called Huguenots settled there, then Germans, Chinese, Vietnamese, Jews and Poles had settled too and the latest arrivals were Caribbeans, Africans, Asians and Bosnians.

Some things never change, though. Every bank holiday the funfair came to Wanstead Flats. All the girls would head there in their girl gangs with their best summer clothes on and the boy gangs would gather with their tough faces and their egos turned on full.

This year Natalie decided to visit the fair with a couple of girlfriends from school, leaving the Gang of Three to themselves. She had gone to the fair before with the boys and she had hated it. All they wanted to do was drive bumper cars, try to win money or stand around posing and trying to look cool. Natalie loved the thrill of the rides, which the boys weren't that keen on, so she wasn't going to let them hold her back.

When the Gang of Three arrived at the fair early in the evening, it was still bright and busy. The sounds of the fair rang out over the Flats and the strange smells of electricity and candyfloss lingered in the air. There was a heavier than usual police presence. It was normal to see a couple of vans in the back streets nearby but tonight there were two vans at the entrance, and extra police on foot.

You could tell that Martin was about to play a prank. He put on his 'mischievous' face. He raised his eyebrows and rubbed his chin. His nostrils flared as if to send more oxygen to his brain, then he smiled. 'You two wait here, watch me.'

Martin walked over to a police officer and started to act distressed. He was very convincing. 'Officer, there's a man over there with a gun!'

The policeman reached for his radio. 'Where, son?'

Martin pointed. 'Over there, officer.'

The officer, who was in a state of full alert, turned, only to find a man pointing a rifle at a coconut shy.

'Hit one coconut and ya get a coconut, hit two and ya get a toy, and if ya hit three ya get a cash prize of a fiver. Can't be bad, good luck, mate,' shouted the vendor on the other side of the counter.

The police officer was furious but relieved. 'Come here, you,' he shouted to Martin, who was acting cool as he tried to walk away. Martin turned back; Matthew and Mark cautiously headed in his direction to listen in.

'What da hell do ya think yu doing? Do you wanna spend time in a cell?'

'What for?'

'What for? How about wasting police time, or giving false information for a start.'

Martin put on his 'reasonable' face. 'What's the matter? Can't ya tek a joke?'

The policeman got angrier and began to point his radio at Martin's face.

'Listen, son, what you just done is no joke. If I'd got on my radio there could have been up to a hundred officers on this spot within a minute. If you think that's a joke, tell me what's funny about it. Think yourself lucky, lad, I got bigger fish to catch than you tonight. Let me tell ya something, if you ever come my way again I'll nick ya, even if I have to nick ya for spitting. I'll lock you up quick, geezer, now move!'

Martin's face was expressionless. He wasn't frightened, in fact he was tempted to laugh to show the other two how in control he was, but he didn't want to upset the officer too much. Matthew looked worried and Mark looked impressed. At this point a small group of onlookers had began to gather and a higher-ranking police officer joined his colleague and asked if there was any trouble.

'No, Sarge, just a kid messing around.'

Matthew grabbed Martin by the wrist and pulled him away. 'Let's go.'

The police officer repeated his warning. 'Remember now, if I see your face near me again, make sure you're innocent.'

Martin was proud of his prank. He checked his credibility with Mark. 'That was cool, wasn't it?'

'Wicked, guy, you got guts,' Mark replied.

Matthew saw things differently. 'You're mad – you can't mess with the law, you know – you're crazy. That's a copper, not a teacher.'

Martin put on his 'victorious' face and proclaimed, 'The law is an ass.'

As the gang ventured further into the fair it became even more apparent that something was not right. Martin stopped two local boys as they passed. 'Hey, man, how come there's so many cops out?'

'There's been trouble,' one of the boys replied.

'The Stokie Crew came down and started to pick pockets. A couple of them tried to mess with Big E girls, so a Big E brother pull a knife and Stokie Crew have to run.'

'Any bloodshed?' Mark enquired.

'Nah, when the Stokie boys see blade, them disappear.'

'Later,' Martin ended and the two groups went their ways.

The Big E was the Big E Posse, E meaning East, an alliance of East End gangs. Once all the gangs in the East End fought each other, white gangs, black gangs, Muslim gangs, Sikh gangs and Chinese gangs. But when they were all under attack from gangs like the Stokie Crew from Stoke Newington in North London and the South London Massive, they were forced to unite and defend Newham, their piece of East London. When united they were left alone and no blood was shed.

Big gangs still existed on the East Side like the Tigers, the Dread Lions and also school gangs like the Big Six Posse and the Soul Crew but they were all affiliated to the Big E Posse.

Today it seemed that the Stokie Crew had been sent back to North London but the police weren't taking any chances.

CHAPTER 3

~ Street Life ~

It was a hot, sticky Saturday night and East London was alive. Every car stereo was turned to the full, every convertible car was converted and every house that had a fan was burning up electricity. Every fifteen minutes or so sirens could be heard in the distance – and some not so distant. People took it for granted that whatever was going down had nothing to do with them. All they had to do was get out of the way and stay composed as they did so. Even the police looked relaxed tonight: those that were on the cruise had their windows down, shirtsleeves up and radios blasting out – police radio that is, talk radio.

At home Martin had just finished his bath. He stood in his bedroom looking at himself in the full-length mirror making sure his old Kappa sweatshirt and baseball cap went with the Armani jeans that his mother had just bought him. But he wasn't sure about his trainers. Could he wear a pair of cheap Hi-Tec trainers with his £50 worth of sweatshirt and his £90 worth of jeans? It didn't look right. Then he realised that he didn't have any other trainers anyway. The doorbell rang once, ding-dong, then twice, ding-dong, then there was a continuous ding-dong, ding-dong, ding-dong. Martin ran down the stairs jumping three steps at a time and sounding like a herd of elephants.

His mother shouted from the living room, 'Martin, tell ya friend that there's no one here with a hearing problem. One bloody ring is enough – and walk downstairs, will ya.'

When Martin opened the door he found Mark and Matthew trying to keep a straight face. 'Why ya ringing the bell so much, man. My parents are watching television, man.'

Mark stopped laughing. 'What's the problem? That's the way ya ring my bell.'

'Yeah but not if yu parents are in.'

'Dat's how yu ring it all the time, guy.'

'I don't, man, I look for ya dad's car first,' Martin said, pointing to the road.

'My dad doesn't always drive, yu know, guy. Anyway, ya don't even know my dad's car.'

'Course I do.'

'What is it, den?'

'It's a Ford.'

'Look, how many different Fords there are. What kind of Ford?'

Matthew interrupted, 'Forget it, let's go.'

Martin shouted back into the flat, 'Mom, Dad, I'm off out. I'll see ya later.'

'Hang on a minute.' Martin's mother forced herself to leave the murder mystery she was watching and made her way to the hallway. 'Now you lot, look after yourselves and don't go getting yourselves into trouble. Any problems give us a ring, all right . . . and Martin, look after those jeans, they cost a bloody bomb, I should have insured them.'

Mark and Matthew muttered, 'Yes, Mrs Turner,' holding back the laughter.

Martin felt obliged to answer. 'Yes, Mom, we're safe, don't worry and if there's any problems with my jeans, I'll ring.'

'Go on, get out.'

As they approached Natalie's house they walked very slowly, knowing that she would be looking out for them. Martin promised that he would not call attention to himself or look in but he couldn't help having a peep. He called Natalie's father Sherlock, after Sherlock Holmes, because he always wore tweed and he always had a pipe hanging from his mouth, which he never seemed to smoke.

As Martin looked in, there was Sherlock, reading a newspaper on his puffy chair. His chair was placed so that he could watch television and the world outside the window at the same time. It looked as if her mother was asleep on the settee and he could not see Natalie. They walked past, stopped at the corner and after a small debate on whether they should or shouldn't, they decided to walk past again. As they walked past this time all three looked at once. Natalie's mother and father were still in position but this time Natalie was there, standing above her father, looking straight back at them. She hurried them on with a slight flick of her eyes and they were gone.

By the time they reached the other corner Natalie was out of the house and walking down behind them. She was wearing clothes that shone, light green satin trousers and a frilly dark green satin blouse with plat-form shoes that weren't quite platform shoes but platform trainers.

Her hair was tied back in a ponytail and she was not wearing a smile. 'I told you lot not to look in my house. What if my dad sees you?'

It was Martin's job to reply. 'We couldn't see ya, and anyway we were careful.'

'You weren't careful, you were all staring into my house as if someone in there owed you money.'

'Come on, take it easy, you know I love you.'

'Love what? Where are we going then?'

Martin looked at Matthew, Matthew looked at Mark then all three looked at Natalie and shrugged their shoulders. Natalie raised her voice. 'Hope you ain't brought me out here to walk the streets.'

'No way, I wouldn't let my girl walk the streets all night. We just gonna walk to kill a bit of time, then we going to a nice club where you will be wined and dined, man.'

'Man, why do you always say "man"?' said Natalie. 'If you're a man, that means I'm a woman and even so, I ain't YOUR woman, I am me.'

Mark tried to lighten the conversation. 'Yeah, girl power.'

Natalie was abrupt. 'Shut up, you.'

An outsider would have been fooled but none of them took this conversation seriously. They all laughed out loud and began to walk. The walk was a lazy, slow one; there was no breeze, so after ten minutes on the move the sweat broke out and their clothes began to stick to their skin. They stopped first outside the fried chicken shop on Green Street, but no one wanted to eat.

Mark, Martin and Matthew spotted four boys from Eastmorelands and headed over to say hello. This was not Natalie's scene at all. She knew that she couldn't afford to look timid, so she lifted her shoulders and held her head high as she stood around listening to the boys' small talk.

After a couple of minutes she realised that her every move was being watched by a group of three girls and she couldn't help noticing how tough they looked. All three were wearing dark blue baggy jeans. She was pretty sure they were Londoners born and bred but thought that they could find a job working for the Jamaican tourist board, not simply because of their dark skin but also because of their clothing. One had a T-shirt saying 'I Love Jamaica'. Another wore a T-shirt that was a Jamaican flag and the third just had a West Ham football shirt on, but she, like the others, was adorned with yellow, black and green bangles, badges and necklaces. Natalie thought they looked good but dangerous.

Natalie shifted nervously. She didn't know quite where to look but she had to put on a front. The other three girls made no attempt to hide the fact that they were on Natalie's case. They began to whisper to each other and smile as they stared at her. Natalie felt illuminated in her green satins and began to wish she had chosen clothes that weren't so loud. *What are they grinning at?* she wondered. *Is it my clothes? My shoes? My hair? Do I look too innocent?* Suddenly the three girls started to walk towards Natalie. Her heart began to race, the palms of her hands began to sweat. She felt like falling apart but she held herself together.

'You from round here, den?' said the girl wearing the big Jamaican flag.

'Yeah.'

'What school yu go to, den?'

'Eastmorelands.'

'Yeah, I wanid ta go there but they wouldn't let me, said I had ta go ta Lonsdale Park, said it was nearer. What ya doing here?'

The two other girls continued to look her up and down. Natalie expected trouble and in her mind she cursed the boys for bringing her there and for the way they had got lost in their silly conversation about football and cars.

'I'm just hanging around with me boyfriend and his mates.'

At this point the girl wearing the West Ham shirt reached into her back pocket. Natalie swallowed hard as the girl pulled out a couple of leaflets. After separating one from the other she handed one to Natalie. 'Dat's the place to be, check it out, good vibes, good music. Ya like rap?'

Natalie wanted to kick herself. She had completely misread the situation. These girls weren't out for a fight, they wanted to find out if she liked clubbing. They wanted to find out if she was one of them, an Eastender.

'Yeah,' Natalie replied, feeling a sense of relief. 'Yeah, rap's cool, I used to love MC Lucky till he got all serious. Now I'm into the Tribe and stuff like that.'

'Me too, I love the Tribe. If yu like the Tribe, you'll like dis place, dis place is great for rap tunes. Try and make it down there if you can, see ya later maybe. It's girls free before ten.'

With that all three turned around and went into the fried chicken shop.

The Gang of Three were rounding off their conversation behind Natalie. Natalie was still recovering. She began to wonder if she sometimes looked threatening and if she herself had been misjudged by people in the past. For people to be friendly, did they have to have permanent smiles on their faces?

Martin joined her with the other two following. 'Who were they?'

'Who?'

'Those black girls you were talking to.'

'Me friends.'

'I didn't know you had black friends.' Martin spoke in almost a whisper.

'I haven't got black friends,' she replied firmly. 'I've just got friends.'

Martin looked around and again in a whisper he said, 'Hush.'

Martin knew that there was no way he would get away with a racist remark here. The group they had been talking to had ethnic origins that ranged from the Philippines, to Africa and Bosnia and he was not going to upset any of them.

'Let's make a move,' he said.

They walked down Green Street. Green Street was a street with two personalities. By day it was a shopping area, at night clubbers used its kebab houses, restaurants and Indian take-aways. Groups gathered on corners.

As they walked, Martin tried to guess the smells he came across: fish and chips, curries, pizza and kebabs. Not being an imaginative eater, he got many of them wrong but it was sometimes hard to distinguish smells in places where they all seemed to meet. As they passed the various butchers, all of them played dodge the chicken heads. He remembered how Green Street was described as the heart of the Asian community in a school project that he had done on local history. He picked out Chinese shops, African dress shops, a Filipino bookshop, shops that sold jellied eels, Jamaican breads and Somalian foods. Then he saw a reminder of the sadder side of life in this area. Many of the shops had metal shutters on their windows and doors to protect them from racist attacks. But here racists had even attacked the shutters. Some of the shutters had racist graffiti painted on them and others had scorch marks left after fire bomb attacks.

At the end of Green Street there was a massive police station that towered way above the other buildings. Martin stopped and looked up at it. 'Forest Fortress. I hate this place.'

Natalie quizzed him. 'What do you hate, the place or the people in it?'

'I don't care about the people in it, man. Just look

at that building, it's the most uninviting building I've ever seen.'

Mark looked up at the dull red brickwork. 'It's a cop shop, cop shops ain't supposed to look inviting. It's supposed to be a symbol of authority.'

'You mean state oppression,' Martin replied. 'The papers said thousands and thousands of pounds been spent on this place – can't they make state oppression or authority look pretty, man?'

Natalie gently slapped Martin around the back of his head. 'What do you know about state oppression, stupid?'

Next door to the police station was 'Prizes Galore'. Outside it said '**Amusement Arcade**' but in truth it was just an old shoe shop with a couple of gambling machines in it. When Natalie and the Gang of Three arrived it was packed out and not one of the gamblers in there was over 18. Even the girl giving out the change looked underage. Here there was no such thing as silence; the machines constantly buzzed and bleeped. A pinball machine in one corner let out a *Hammer Horror* style howl every two minutes if no one played it, whilst in another corner a fruit machine shaped like a woman actually spoke. 'Play me, play me, play me.' Together they walked around, watching the games that were being played. When Martin heard the fruit machine calling *play me*, his eyes lit up with excitement. 'I'll play you,' he exclaimed.

Natalie put herself between him and the machine. 'No, cause I know once you get playing we're gonna be stuck here all night – and how much money you got anyway?'

'Ah, don't worry, I got money and I only want one game.'

Mark took a good look at the machine and laughed. 'He just fancies her.'

Matthew agreed. 'Yeah, hey, don't be fooled, Martin, she's only after your money.'

Martin began to search his pockets for change but Natalie wouldn't give him a chance.

'Come on, let's go, I'm not staying here.'

Martin put on his 'puzzled' face and asked, 'What's up?'

'OK den, you stay, I'm going somewhere else.' With that Natalie headed for the door.

Martin raised his eyebrows and turned to follow her. Mark and Matthew followed him.

Outside the arcade Mark took control. 'Right. Where we going den? We're just wasting time, let's go somewhere good.'

'I know,' Matthew replied. 'Let's go to the Unity Club.'

Martin was quick to interrupt. 'No way, man, that place is for soft kids. Table tennis, pool, tiddlywinks – that's no way to spend your Saturday night.'

The Unity Club was a youth club in a church run

by a priest named Tony. In reality the Unity was not the coolest place to go, but the kids in the area sometimes used it as a meeting place and as somewhere to shelter from the rain.

'Yeah, you're right,' Matthew acknowledged. 'We should go somewhere where there's music.'

Martin's face lit up. 'I've got an idea, a good one as usual. Let's go to dis new rave club. It's called Psycho and it's just on Forest Road.'

Mark was never keen on rave music. 'Nah, rave music, boff boff, bang bang, all night and the people are weird.'

Matthew agreed. 'Yeah, last time I went to one of dem raves up in Ilford, someone tried to sell me drugs every five minutes.'

Martin started to defend his idea but he sensed that he had already lost this one. 'There's drugs everywhere, man, everywhere ya go there's dealers.'

'Yeah, but those rave places are crazy on Es and at least in other places ya not getting it every five minutes.'

Martin gave up and turned to Natalie, who was reading the leaflet given to her outside the fried chicken shop. 'That's it,' she said, 'let's go there, only three pounds entrance, ladies free before ten.'

'What kind of sounds?' Mark enquired.

'Rap,' Natalie replied.

Martin put on his 'disgusted' face. 'RAP!' He moved close to Natalie, took a corner of the leaflet and read it out loud.

31

He looked at Natalie. 'I'm not going there, it's all black music.'

Natalie was outraged. 'What you on about – nearly all music's black music. What do you know?'

'The place is gonna be full of blacks, they don't like us . . . OK, some like us but not in their clubs.'

'I'm fed up of you, if you don't come with me I'm

32

going there on my own, I got friends there.'

Martin couldn't quite believe what he was hearing but he could tell that she meant it. Mark tried to make peace. 'It's only three pounds each and we all got over three pounds, so let's go. If we don't like it, we'll move on. I reckon it'll be OK!'

'Me too,' Matthew agreed. 'Anyway, Martin, what you got against blacks? No black's ever hurt you.'

'I ain't got nothing against blacks, they're just different, they dance different and everything.'

Natalie walked away from the group and called Martin over to her. 'If you don't like someone just because they're different you got problems. What do ya expect, everyone to be like **you**? Maybe you should have went out with Pat James, she doesn't like anyone.'

'Do you think dat's funny?'

'No, I'm not messing, if you keep on like this I won't go out with you anymore. Yu gotta respect people and if you don't wanna go to the rap club don't force yourself but I'm going.'

'Ya really serious?'

'Yeah.'

Martin got the message loud and clear. As they joined Mark and Matthew he proclaimed in a mediocre rap style,

'*OK, you guys,*
me and you and the girl I love
are going to

the rap club.'

Mark was surprised by his quick change of mind. 'Are you OK, mate?'

'Yeah, man, rap's cool.'

CHAPTER 4

~ Dancemania ~

They arrived at Dancemania with ten minutes to go before ten o'clock. Martin couldn't help noticing how big the two bouncers were who stood at the door and how they looked like identical twins. The counter staff and the other club goers all looked big too. To his surprise they weren't all black.

At the youth club dances and the raves that he had been to in the past, most of the people were around his age. At these places he was quite well known. But here he was just like anyone else. He felt a sense of adventure, like going into an unknown world.

Mark and Matthew handed their three pounds each to their leader Martin and he paid the entrance fees. This gave him a feeling of importance. The woman taking the money just waved Natalie on and they were in. The dance floor was packed with bodies moving to the music. There was no order. This was freestyle with people dancing any way they wanted to. A cloud of tobacco smoke hung just below the ceiling. Martin thought that the way the lights impacted on the smoke made the place look heavenly.

The four newcomers stared into the dance floor. The music was as loud as the raves that they were accustomed to but the outstanding feature with this sound system was the bass. The floor shivered with the bass notes and even though the four had not fully acclimatised yet, they could not stop themselves from nodding their heads and tapping their feet to the beat. The bass made sure of that, it was unnatural to fight it.

Natalie felt someone gently pull her ponytail. It was one of the girls from the fried chicken shop, the one wearing the Jamaican flag. She had to shout directly into Natalie's ear to be heard. 'So ya made it, den?'

'Yeah.' Not having spoken since being inside the club Natalie did not realise how easy it was for words to get lost.

'Pardon?'

'I said YEAH,' Natalie shouted.

'Which one's ya boyfriend, den?'

Natalie pointed to Martin, who by now was nodding frantically to a record by the rapper Freak Froggy Frog.

'Does he like rap, den?'

'He does now,' Natalie replied with a smile on her face.

'Come here and meet me home girls.'

'Meet your who?' Natalie shouted.

'Me home girls, me crew, me frens.'

Natalie signalled the three to follow her and they followed Natalie's new friends to a corner of the club where the music was just a couple of decibels lower than on the dance floor.

The painted brick walls covered with condensation made it look as if even the walls were sweating. This corner was more relaxed, people came here to chill out or cool down when things got too hot. The other two girls that Natalie had met outside the fried chicken shop were drinking beer and looking out for people they knew. As the two groups met they greeted each other with a nod. Not a word was spoken until Matthew felt that he had to say something and exercise his tongue.

He leant over to Natalie. 'Hey Natalie, introduce us to ya friends, I feel stupid.'

Natalie leaned over to the girl wearing the Jamaican flag. 'What's your names?'

She gathered them all together into a tight little circle and they introduced themselves to each other. The Jamaican flag girl was called Marica. She was the small one, only five foot and a great basketball player. The girl wearing the *I Love Jamaica* T-shirt had just returned from Jamaica with her parents. This was the reason for all the Jamaican paraphernalia. Her name was Tina but everyone called her *Teen*. The tallest of the three was called Nasreen which meant Jericho Rose. When she first told Marica and Teen what her name meant they began to call her *Jericho Rose* and she hated it, so they now called her *Naz*. Because of her height people always thought she was a basketball player but she hated basketball and was crazy about West Ham United Football Club.

A couple of attempts were made to strike up some conversation but the volume of the music only allowed a few words to be said at a time. An exchange of ideas or a debate on a theory was very difficult.

For the next couple of records, everyone stood around nodding their heads to the music. Teen left the group and quickly returned with two large cans of beer. She pulled the rings and opened both cans. After taking a sip from one she passed it to Marica, then she took a sip from the other can and passed it to Martin.

Natalie leaned over to Martin and shouted over the music. 'What are you doing? You don't drink.'

Martin smiled and replied back loudly, 'This ain't drinking. Two cans between seven people, you can't get drunk on that.'

'You can,' she insisted.

'Don't be silly.'

Martin put the can to his mouth and took a really big gulp before he handed it to Natalie. 'Just have a sip, it won't hurt you.'

Natalie took a small sip and passed it on to Naz.

Naz took a sip and passed it on to Mark. And so the two cans circulated around the group before ending up empty on the ground. Martin drank a lot. Mark tried to look like he had drunk a lot. Matthew drank very little and Natalie had two minute sips. Soon Martin was really getting into the music, and now he was not just watching but admiring some of the dancers on the floor. He noticed that Natalie and her friends were happily dancing away as if they had been friends for years.

Martin couldn't contain himself any longer. He turned his basketball cap backwards and hit the dance floor. His head was doing fine, on the beat every time. Now he had to get the rest of his body to work. He started with a stepping backwards and forwards move-ment which worked – he looked around to make sure no one disapproved. From there he added a sideways step that seemed to work, and he continued with a one, two, forward, a one, two, back, one, two, left, one, two, right trip which meant that he commanded even more space and still no one complained – the fact that he got the room he needed was a sign that he deserved it. After a minute he realised that he had to do more, it was becoming a bit routine and his hands weren't doing much, so he took all the steps and applied the chaos theory, going forward, then left, then backwards, then left, then forward, then right, any way at all. Then he put his hands in the air and . . .

PANIC!!! *No one else has their hands in the air*, he thought. *Do I look like a raver? I don't want to look like a raver in here.* At this point he noticed a couple of people looking. His hands were still in the air but he didn't want his concerns to be known, so he moved his hands from side to side and whilst he was doing that he lost the rhythm in his feet.

Now he really began to panic. He screamed internally, *Oh, no, I look like Cliff Richard, I'm dancing like my parents.* The more he tried to return to his credible steps and find something useful to do with his hands, the more he thought he'd lost it. *No, they're looking at me*, he said to himself. *What can I do with my hands?*

In front of him he saw somebody dancing and adding gymnastic moves to the dance. *That's it*, Martin thought, *I can do that*. His feet found the rhythm and he chose his beat well. When it hit he went down for the splits and bounced back. It worked. He counted in his head, *one, two, three* and lounged forward as if he was going to fall on his face and at the last minute he put his hands forward to cushion himself. Now the other gymnastic dancer noticed and came to dance in front of Martin, copying his moves and falling at his feet. The crowd made a space and Martin realised they were now the central attraction. The boy went down into the splits position and put both his hands on the floor to his left, then he bounced again, bringing his hands to the right as he came down, then he rolled forward head-first on to his feet, and as he landed he was still dancing with his hands on his hips.

The crowd clapped. Martin looked around and there was Marica, Natalie, Naz and Teen bopping to the beat and looking on. 'Go on, Martin, do ya stuff,' came a shout from behind. It was Mark.

Matthew stood silent, suffering from disbelief. Martin dropped into the splits with his hands to the left, then to the right. He then put his hands one to each side and picked himself up. After a little fancy footwork he dropped down again, spun himself around and rolled forward head-first on to his feet. This was enough to get the crowd going, but then to everyone's astonishment Martin moonwalked backwards, took two steps forwards and somersaulted. He landed perfectly, finishing in a muscle man pose.

The crowd loved it, they cheered and reached out to touch the two dancers. The two dancers slapped hands in the air and went their separate ways. It was a friendly competition and not a word had been passed between the two dancers. There was rapturous applause from the crowd and Martin, now the cool white brother, had earned some respect.

Natalie and her friends made their way back to their corner. The Gang of Three followed after Martin had received all his congratulations and what felt like a hundred pats on his back. Natalie was speechless – less than two hours ago he didn't like rap. In the past when she saw him dancing he looked as if he was being forced – now he was the star of the show.

Marica didn't know all this of course. 'Hey man, ya didn't say ya boyfriend was a dance champ.'

Martin decided to be honest. 'I can't dance, I'm just good at gymnastics.'

'I've got over a hundred witnesses, you just rocked the house,' Marica shouted.

It was Naz and Teen's turn. Martin couldn't tell who was saying what as the compliments rained down on him.

'Yu bad guy.'

'Yeah man, ya wicked.'

'De cool ruler.'

'Cool and easy does it.'

Martin was on top of the world. Going from a nobody to being the main attraction had done his ego a world of good. His credibility was sealed and Natalie was proud of him.

Matthew looked at his watch. It was now after midnight and he was beginning to feel tired. He was never much of a clubber and even though he was enjoying himself, his eyelids were beginning to feel heavy. He was sitting at a table with Mark. Martin was still standing, nodding his head and trying desperately to understand what these rap lyrics meant. The alcohol did not help him to make out what all these

American rap artists were saying.

Matthew was beginning to really feel the pressure. The noise and the smoke were getting to him but he didn't want to spoil it for the others.

Then he heard a voice from behind. 'How ya doing, mate?'

Matthew turned and looked behind him. It was a man who he did not know, with a tattoo on his neck and short blonde hair. He was dressed in a brown three-piece suit and the first thing that came to Matthew's mind was the heat. *How could he stand it in that suit?*

The man leaned down to Matthew until his lips were almost touching his ear. 'I got Es at prices no one can beat and if you're into a bit of coke or smack, give me fifteen minutes and I can do ya a bargain.'

Matthew looked around him. In the corner the girls were dancing and all smiles, Martin was into the beats and Mark was practically asleep. Matthew stood up. 'Piss off, mate.'

'Who ya talkin to?' the pusher replied.

'You, ya bastard. Piss off.'

The pusher put his hand in his pocket and they looked into each other's eyes. Matthew was scared but he had to stand his ground. He thought the pusher could have a knife or even a gun in his pocket – or he could also be calling his bluff. They stared each other in the eyes for twenty seconds. The pusher was the first one to look away, checking to see if they had been noticed by anyone else. All around them life carried on as normal. 'Don't mess with me, schoolboy, cause I don't mess. I cut flesh like you!' he said with a menacing growl.

Matthew still wouldn't back down. 'Piss off.' The pusher turned away and disappeared into the crowd.

Matthew stood up. He pushed Mark, startling him, 'Get up, come on.'

Then he walked over to Martin. 'Come on, I'm going.'

Martin was confused. 'What's happening, man?'

Mark was just as puzzled. 'I dunno, I ain't done nothing.'

The three went to get Natalie, who tried to convince Matthew to stay but he wouldn't. He would only say that *he would tell them later*. Marica, Teen and Naz sensed that something had happened to cause them to act this way but they weren't going to ask questions now.

'Listen,' Marica said, 'we be down here next week so come down if ya can, check some more grooves. Weekdays sometimes we out by the chicken shop. Stay cool.'

'See ya,' and Natalie followed the boys out of the club.

CHAPTER 5

~ Crash ~

Martin, Mark, Matthew and Natalie headed down the street in silence for a while until Natalie opened the debate. 'I was enjoying dat, good club dat. What's up with you lot?'

Matthew told them the story of the drug pusher. Martin reminded him of something that he had said earlier. 'Well I told ya, there are druggies everywhere.'

'Yeah,' Matthew replied, 'but this guy was a creep and I was tired and I wasn't in the mood for geezers like that.'

As they continued to walk, Martin's dance routine became the main topic of conversation. 'I wasn't sure of that place at first,' Martin confessed as if no one had known. 'But it's OK – I'm into those rap beats.'

Natalie was pleased with herself. 'I knew you'd like it,' she said as she linked her arm into Martin's. 'I had a great time – I'll be back.'

When they arrived at the top of Natalie's street,

Mark and Matthew waited on the corner while Martin walked her down a little. He had to make sure she got home safe but he also had to make sure he got his goodnight kiss. At a convenient spot he stopped. He had done this before but he still didn't know what to say, so he said the first thing that came into his head. 'Where do ya mom and dad think you are?'

'Well, I told them I was going to the Unity with some girlfriends,' she grinned.

Martin wasted no more time. He reached round the back of her head, pulled her towards him, and kissed her. But it wasn't a real kiss. All he was doing was putting his lips against hers and pushing. There was no tenderness at all.

Natalie tolerated it for a few seconds and then pushed him away. 'I told you, you can kiss me if you ask first.'

Martin was panting. He had been holding his breath while kissing, now he was out of breath and overexcited. 'OK, OK den, gissa kiss.'

He kissed her again. This time she took control and put her tongue in his mouth. Martin started to run his hands through her hair, then up and down her back, and then his hands headed in all directions as if desperately seeking lost flesh.

'Ouch,' Martin shouted down Natalie's throat. Natalie had stamped on his foot. Martin spoke, even though they were still connected at the lips. 'What did you do that for?'

'Stop ya from going too far.'

Mark and Matthew were on the corner, observing the ritual whilst trying not to be caught looking. Natalie and Martin struggled on, but it was too much for Martin. Soon the tongue went to his head and off went his hands again.

'OUCH!' This time it was the other foot.

Natalie pulled away. 'I've got to go now. I'll ring ya tomorrow.'

Martin pleaded, 'Gissa nother kiss.'

'I'll give ya a kiss tomorrow if ya teach me some of them dance moves.'

'Yeah, it's a deal, ya got yourself a deal there, girl.'

He kissed her hand and watched her open her front door and enter before he moved off up the road where he found Mark and Matthew acting as if they had seen nothing.

The Gang of Three decided to cut through the Monega Estate in order to get back on to Green Street. It was now one o'clock and the big boys were out.

The Gang of Three knew this estate well. In the 1970s it used to be a good-looking estate where people wanted to be but now it needed some attention. One of the high-rise buildings had no entrance doors on either the front or back. Like thousands before them, the gang just walked straight through. Martin glanced at the stairway as he passed and in a split second he noticed condom packets and glue containers on the steps. As they came out of the rear door space, used needles left by drug addicts lay on the floor. Martin crushed one under his foot.

Matthew was disgusted. 'I wouldn't even step on one of them – say if one went through your sole? Could give you AIDS.'

As they walked through the centre of the estate, they heard the sound of screeching tyres, the sound of a car being raced. It was just a block away and they could smell the burning rubber. The sound moved away from them but then they heard the car turn, and the sound started heading their way. All three stepped on to a square paved area in the middle of the road where two of the small estate roads met and where once a bollard had stood. Then out of the dark they saw a set of headlights approaching. The lights were on full beam, so they couldn't see the make of the car or the driver, and it was coming fast and revving hard. The car went past the three, just missing them, then turned back towards them. Martin looked up at the high-rise flats and was amazed to find that there were no angry tenants cursing out of their windows. Mark was fearful and Matthew was just aggravated.

The car pulled up at the side of the concrete island. The smell of the burning tyres entered their nostrils and caused all their eyes to water. The sound of the engines revving up made all three cover their ears for a moment, until the driver let the engine tick over.

A shout came from the car. 'Martin, Mark!'

Martin bent down to look at the vehicle. He didn't recognise the driver.

'Martin, man, it's me, Pete.'

Martin looked into the front passenger seat and then saw the face behind the voice. It was Peter Mosley. He used to go to Eastmorelands School and was a member of the Big Six gang then. Now he was a member of the Raider's Posse, a gang known for their outlawish activities.

Matthew bent down and looked into the car. 'Why yu mekin up so much noise in people's ears?'

The car was a red Ford Escort. The driver, who was unknown to the three, looked older than Pete. Pete was always out with older members of the gang and had a reputation for carrying all sorts of weapons. Pete shouted, 'Come on, let's go riding.'

'Nah, we're going home,' Martin replied.

'Come on, man, have wheels, will travel.'

Matthew would have none of it. 'Piss off, will ya.'

Pete's voice took on a serious tone as he addressed Matthew. 'You take care bout what you say, weakling, don't go upsetting me now.'

Pete kept trying to persuade the three to get into the car. Eventually he changed tactics. 'All right, ya gotta get to bed, we'll just take ya home.'

Martin began to weaken. 'So you'll just give us a lift home.'

'Yeah.' Pete knew he had cracked him.

Martin was now working for the other side. 'Don't worry, it's just a lift home, we'll be there in five minutes, even less.'

Martin went to the back door of the car and opened it.

Matthew was furious. 'Are you really going? You're mad, you're bloody off ya head.'

Martin looked towards Mark. 'Come on, man.'

Matthew decided that he wasn't hanging around any longer. 'OK, Martin, you go. Mark, it's make your mind up time. I'm off – but I'm telling ya, I think you lot are mad.'

Matthew walked away. Mark looked towards Martin, then towards Matthew and then he walked around the car and got in.

Matthew shouted to his two friends in the car, 'What kind of friends are you two? I thought we supposed to stick together. What happened to Gang of Three unity? All it takes is a troublemaker to appear with a car and unity's gone – well I'm gone.' He turned and headed home.

Martin and Mark were excited. When they had been in cars before they had just gone from A to B in an orderly manner. Now the car was mounting the pavement, speeding over the speed humps, driving on the wrong side of the road and near missing everything. The driver had taken the car down the Barking Road and on to the A13, a major road with three lanes on each side, before Martin realised they were going the wrong way. He had to shout over the engine noise. 'Pete, man, let's turn back.'

Pete didn't care anymore, he was playing drums with his hands on the dashboard. Martin tried again. 'Pete, let's go back, man. What's your mate's name?'

The driver looked about twenty. He had long black hair that went halfway down his back. His upper four front teeth were all gone and he had a scar across his left cheek, all signs of a violent not so long ago. His face was a pale, bloodless white and he smelt like a pub. 'My name's Apache, yeah man, no mercy.'

When he spoke both Martin and Mark could see he was on something. Mark tried to get more information out of him. 'How long ya had the wheels?'

Pete played on the dashboard even harder. Apache began to laugh, a false laugh. Loudly he said, 'Twenty minutes, man, I got dis car twenty minutes ago.'

Martin shot forward. 'What do ya mean, ya nicked it?'

'Look man, this is only a fourteen hundred cc baby. If I was buying one of these it'd be a two thousand. The engine in this thing is just a washing machine engine, I only nicked it cause I can't stand the owner.'

Both Pete and Apache put on tough guy laughs. Martin and Mark looked at each other. Mark shook his head as if to say no and turned to Pete. 'Take us home, just leave us on Green Street. No, never mind Green Street, leave us here.'

The moment he said that Pete called out, 'Coppers, there's cops behind us.'

The police car was tight behind them and flashing its headlights to get them to stop. Apache just put his foot down on the accelerator, speeding forward. The police car stayed right behind him. Martin shouted angrily, 'You bastards, STOP!'

Apache was not listening. His plan was to head back to East Ham, the territory he knew best and try and lose the police in the back streets. As he turned off the A13 main road, Martin saw Pete throw a small package out of the window.

'What's that?' Martin shouted above the roar of the engine.

'I'll show you in five minutes – when we get rid of these pigs, we'll come back for it.'

They were now in a built-up area. The police put on their sirens and flashing lights. Apache and Pete seemed to love the excitement. Martin and Mark were terrified. They sped straight through a red traffic light.

Martin gripped the back of the seat in front of him. 'Let us out. You can do what you wanna do but let us out.'

Mark ranted frantically, 'You won't get away with it, you'll get caught. I'll tell them everything. You didn't tell us that the car was bloody nicked when we got in it.' Taking a deep breath, Mark let out a scream at the top of his voice. 'STOP THE BLOODY CAR, WILL YA.'

Apache and Pete only looked at each other and laughed.

As they approached the junction with Green Street, they could hear more police cars in the distance. The lights were on red and cars were crossing on their right of way.

Mark and Martin shouted, 'STOP! STOP!'

Pete shouted, 'Go for it, man.' As they accelerated across the junction, they were hit. The car rolled over once, throwing Pete out of the front window and sending glass flying. It landed on the opposite side of the road, upside down and was immediately smashed into by a post office van. The car rolled over once more and landed on its wheels.

There was a moment of silence as other drivers looked on in shock. The police car in chase arrived. The two officers from the chase car left their vehicle and approached the wreck in the centre of the crossroads. Apache climbed out of the front window and tried to run, straight into the arms of a police officer.

Mark climbed out of his side window and screamed, 'Help, Martin's in there. My mate's in there.'

He limped around to the other side of the car and tried to open the door but the door was too damaged and would not open. He tried to pull Martin out of the window by his arms. Martin was unconscious. His bloody head just flopped down and Mark was unable to shift Martin's dead weight. A police officer grabbed Mark in a wrist lock and began to lead him away from the car.

Mark protested. 'That's my mate, I'm trying to help my mate.'

'We'll deal with him,' the officer said as he put more pressure on his wrist. The pain was such that Mark was unable to struggle and he was placed in the back of a police car next to Apache.

Apache was rigid with shock. His eyes were fixed straight ahead, he was motionless and emotionless. Blood poured from his ears and the various cuts on his face. Mark had no words for him.

Back at the crashed car, two police officers struggled with their bare hands to try and open the car door to free Martin. Ambulances, more police cars and a fire engine could be heard approaching, their sirens echoing in the night. When they arrived, the police officers ceased their struggle and raced towards the fire engine, knowing that the fire fighters would have cutting equipment. As they did so a loud explosion stopped them in their tracks. Flames licked the interior of the car. The two officers raced back to the car and this time, with all the strength they had left in them they dragged Martin right out of the broken side window. His face was burnt and blackened, his body hung limp and his head rolled lifelessly between their arms. The paramedics laid him on a stretcher, lifted him into an ambulance and rushed him to hospital, whilst the fire fighters used their water hoses to extinguish the fire in the car.

From the back of the police car, Mark shouted as loud as he could, 'That's my mate Martin. I wanna go with him, we're together.' But nobody listened to him.

As the ambulance sped away, Mark fell silent, watching it disappear into the distance. Apache groaned, his head fell forward and he vomited onto the floor of the police car. Tears came to Mark's eyes and he started crying silently.

CHAPTER 6

~ The Awakening ~

Martin began to stir. He woke up slowly. He heard voices close to him. He was still hearing the voices of Mark, Apache and Pete Mosley. There were also the sounds in his brain, buzzing sounds, humming sounds, the sounds of a numbness and dizziness, like a radio in between stations. He kept his eyes closed while he tried to separate the real from the imaginary. Apart from the confusion in his head, he could feel no pain elsewhere on his body – in fact he couldn't even feel his body. He tried to stay calm and attempted to take things step by step. *First my right leg*, he told himself. He consciously instructed his brain to send a message to his right leg but there was no movement. *Now the left leg.* The result was the same. He tried his left arm, then his right arm but there was nothing. For a moment he gave in and tried to listen to the conversation taking place around him.

'I told you ages ago, Clive, I don't like this area. I told you – we should have moved to Upminster long ago.

You can't bring kids up around our end without having to watch them every minute of the day. The drugs, the violence, the lack of respect.'

It was his mother speaking at his father.

'You, you and your mates. You don't want to leave because you would miss your mates. Well, where are your mates now? Half of your mates haven't got kids and if they have got them, they don't know where they are most of the time. There's our kid, lying there.'

Martin began to work it all out as his mind cleared. He began to recall the car chase and its last moments when the car overturned. He could remember the first spin of the car like a slow motion replay. He remembered being trapped upside down after the spin and the noise of being hit by another vehicle, but that was all. Now it began to fall into place. The next question on his mind was, *what has happened to me?* His mother was still talking at his father in the room. She was speaking continuously without a break. Martin began to feel. He actually had a sensation in his fingertips, he began to feel the movement of blood in his veins. He concentrated hard as he tried to move his fingers. Movement was possible but very limited. He was unable to make a fist. As he became aware of his body, he could at least now feel warmth in his limbs.

Very slowly, he began to open his eyes. The hospital lights cut in and forced him to close them again.

He controlled his eyelids, opening them just enough to let his eyes get used to the idea of light. His eyelids flickered. For a moment he stared at his own eyelashes and as he continued his slow opening, he heard a scream.

'Aaarrrgh, Clive, he's waking up, I saw his eyes. Move, Clive, he's waking up.'

'OK, Wendy. It's all right,' Martin's father said in a whisper.

Martin opened his eyes fully. At first he looked straight ahead. He could see clearly but he could not see much, only the hospital ceiling. He closed his eyes once more; now he started a body check. He moved his toes, and tensed his calf muscles and his thigh muscles. He moved his whole left leg no more than a quarter of an inch and then his right leg. It was the smallest of movements but all he wanted to know was that he was in control. By now there was more movement in his fingers, and again, a very small movement of his arms satisfied him. He breathed in deeply and his chest rose. Now Martin opened his eyes again, trying as he did so to raise his eyebrows but there was absolutely no feeling there. He tried to smile but he could feel only a hard skin which he seemed unable to control. He tried to move his jaw from side to side but the skin seemed inflexible and his jaw wouldn't move.

At this point Martin knew that something terrible had happened to his face. His heart pounded hard in his chest. He shifted his eyes to the left and saw his father standing over him.

'Are you OK, son?'

Martin felt that he was using up all his strength just sending blood around his body and opening his eyes – he certainly didn't have the strength to speak. But his mind was beginning to work and he did think that *Are you OK, son?* was a strange question. He had very little idea of how he really was. His mother came into sight on his right side.

'Martin, Martin my baby. We're here, Martin. We're gonna look after you, it's your mom and dad. We're here.'

His mother on one side began to cry uncontrollably, his father on the other side just stared into Martin's eyes. Martin blinked, the blink much slower than he thought it was. By the time he had re-focused, his father was on the same side as his mother with his arms around her. He could see the grief in his eyes and hear the anguish in her crying but he was helpless, unable to move, unable to speak and unable to reach out to her. He gave in. He closed his eyes and fell asleep to the sound of his mother crying above him.

CHAPTER 7

~ The Reality ~

Twenty-four hours later and Martin's parents were back sitting on chairs at each side of the bed. They had been home for a sleepless night and the lack of sleep was beginning to show. His mother had run out of steam and was now as silent as her husband. They both sat looking at Martin as if there was nothing else in the world.

Martin had been given a small side room on the Burns Unit of the Newham Parkside Hospital, the hospital where he had been born fifteen years before. He began to wake up and opened his eyes very slowly. This time he could hear no sound in the room. This time as he looked around the hospital ceiling with its built-in lights, he didn't need to work out where he was and what had brought him there. He was now more aware of himself and he began to feel the pains from the accident. The whole surface of his body felt hot. This time when he tried to move his feet they moved. His mother stood up and calmly looked down over him.

'Martin, love, take it easy. Don't try to move too much.'

His father left the room. His mother struggled to find more words, looking deep into his eyes.

'Don't worry, love, the doctor will be here soon and she'll explain everything to you. Just lie back and relax.'

When his father re-entered the room, he was accompanied by a nurse and doctor. One on each side, they both looked down at him and peered into his eyes before the doctor began to give the nurse instructions.

'OK, Nurse, let's raise him up.'

The nurse began to turn a mechanism at the back of the bed and Martin's torso was lifted up. The view was different now. He could see straight ahead for the first time. All eyes in the room were still on him.

'Put his arms on top of the blankets,' said the doctor, as she reached for Martin's records hanging at the bottom of the bed.

As the nurse gently took Martin's arms from underneath the blanket, Martin looked at her. He wasn't used to strangers moving his limbs around and he wasn't sure if he should be making any effort. The nurse looked Chinese; her eyes were at the same level as his even though she was standing. Martin looked into her eyes, but she was concentrating on her task. She folded the blanket back gently as if the blanket had feelings. The task over, she stepped back awaiting new orders. After a quick look at the report, the doctor replaced it and then walked over to Martin.

'Hello, Martin. This is Nurse Ling and my name is Dr Janet Owens. Now you may want to be left alone for a while – that is completely up to you – but there are some things that we need to talk about. How is your voice?'

Martin uttered his first words: 'All right – I think.' The words fell out of his mouth from the back of his throat without any help from his burnt lips.

The doctor continued. 'Is it OK if I have a word with you now?'

'Yes.' Again the word fell out of his head.

'OK, I am sure that by now you realise how serious the accident was. You were really thrown around when the car rolled and you received a few cuts and lots of bruises to your body but luckily no broken bones. You had two cuts which needed stitches, both on the bottom of your leg, your calf. This is where the car door cut into you. The other cuts will heal themselves so long as we keep them clean. There are some light burns to your hands which should soon heal without treatment.' Dr Owens paused for a moment and surveyed Martin's face. 'But your face came out the worst. You have what we term deeper partial-thickness burns, sometimes called deep dermal burns. At the moment painkillers are holding back the pain but we want to get you off them as soon as we can. In some parts of your face you will feel no pain at all. This is because some of the nerve endings have been severely damaged. You may need some skin grafting. This is where we take skin from one part of your body and move it to your face – but we will only do grafts with your blessing.' She paused and took a deep breath before continuing. 'The drugs may be making you feel very strange right now and you have probably lost track of time. Well, it was early Sunday morning when you had the accident and it's Monday evening now. Have you any questions?'

Martin didn't reply.

He had been listening intensively, and all he could think about was the seriousness of his injuries. He could feel his heart racing. He found it hard to believe that he had been unconscious for a whole day.

The doctor continued, 'I have two other important things to say to you. Firstly, sooner or later you will see the severity of your burns. You must prepare yourself for this. Don't be too alarmed: remember that over time we can improve things. And secondly, a hospital counsellor will come to visit you soon. He is here to help you in anyway he can. Don't be afraid to speak to him on any subject. He – in fact – we – are all here for you if you need us. I'll be seeing you again tomorrow. Then we can talk about your treatment in much more detail.'

All Martin could manage in reply was, 'Thank . . . you.' His ears seemed only half awake, sounds and voices had lost their sharpness and were muffled. For the first time in his life he wanted to cry but he didn't have any tears.

The doctor asked Mr and Mrs Turner if she could speak with them outside and everyone left the room. There was silence. Martin turned slowly to the right. It took him a long time, it was like viewing the world through a camera lens. The walls were a cream colour and bare. As he looked down and to his side he saw a brown, bedside table with nothing on it and a console with light switches and radio controls. It took him another twenty seconds to turn to his left, only to find another creamy wall with a single towel hanging from a holder. Bold lettering on the towel read 'Property of Newham Parkside Hospital'. The room was small with a chair at each side of his bed. Martin spent the next few minutes looking at as much of the room as his injured body allowed. He began to wonder what had happened to the others in the car. He wondered where Mark was. He just could not imagine what had happened to Apache and Pete. He thought of Matthew, he thought of Natalie and then once more he fell asleep.

When he woke up it was Tuesday morning. His parents were standing together at the side of his bed. He noticed that they were holding hands. He had now seen them hugging *and* holding hands. He couldn't remember seeing them holding hands before, only in photographs taken before he was born.

His mother went to the bottom of his bed and wheeled a food trolley towards him. On the tray was a bowl of soup with a straw.

'Here you are, Martin, a bit of warm soup for you. You need it.'

'No,' Martin replied. 'I don't want any.'

'Come on, Martin,' his mother insisted. 'It will do you good.'

Martin put the straw in the soup bowl and tried to drink. He was aware of every drop as it entered his dry mouth, and slid down his parched throat into his empty stomach. The soup was tasteless. He tried to like it. After a couple of mouthfuls, he made a gentle protest.

'I can't, Mom. Take it away.'

Reluctantly his mother wheeled it away. 'Do try some more later, you need it to build up your strength.'

Nurse Ling and a male nurse entered the room. His mother squeezed his hand gently.

'We have to go now, we'll be back later.'

Martin took a deep breath and spoke his first short but full sentence. 'Where are you going?'

'The nurse needs to see you now and we have to go home. We'll be back later and we'll bring you some things.'

'Don't worry, son,' his father said as they left the room. His father had always been a man of few words and in times of grief his words were even fewer. He looked dazed and shell-shocked. He just seemed to be following his wife around, listening to all that she, the doctors and the nurses had to say, only responding when necessary. 'See you later, son.' He always called Martin 'son'.

Nurse Ling smiled at Martin. 'Hi, Martin. Now we have a job to do which means moving you around a little. It won't take long. All we have to do is change the bandages on your stitches. OK?'

'OK,' he replied, unsure of what this meant. *Would it be a painful experience or did it just sound painful?*

Together the nurses folded back the blanket and sheets and removed the hospital issue pyjamas that he was wearing. Martin watched their every move. For the first time he was seeing the damage done to his legs. They were covered with small cuts, scratches and bruises. The bruises varied in colour from red to blue to purple. The two bandages were on the outside of his left calf, one low, and one high. The bloodstains on the white bandages worried Martin at first but as the bandages were slowly removed by Nurse Ling he relaxed – in the event it was quite painless. New bandages were put on, as were new pyjamas, and soon the nurses were on their way out. But Martin's mind began to work quickly. He had now seen the injuries on his body. *Why not his face?*

'Nurse,' he shouted.

'Yes, Martin.'

'Can I have a mirror?'

There was an uneasy pause, while the nurses looked at each other. The male nurse said nothing and Nurse Ling hesitantly replied, 'Well, it's not as easy as that.'

She headed back towards Martin and the male nurse left the room. 'The hospital has to be very careful about this and we can't just give mirrors out on request. Give me a couple of minutes and I'll see what I can do.' She gave him a warm smile and left the room.

Martin began to prepare himself. He thought that he might have a battle to fight here but he had made up his mind: he wanted to see his face.

Five minutes later, a man entered the room. He was casually dressed in a shirt and jeans with long black hair which he wore in a ponytail. He looked so cool and relaxed that Martin thought he was a visiting pop star.

The man smiled. He walked over to Martin and sat on his bed. 'Hi, my name's Alan, Alan Green, but just call me Alan.' He was softly spoken with a Scottish accent. 'My official title is Clinical Psychologist but even I don't like that, it makes me sound like someone who does experiments. You just think of me as some- one you can talk to if you have any problems. It's completely up to you how you use me. I am not allowed to make a nuisance of myself but on the other hand I am always here when you need me, or I'll try to be.'

Martin was surprised by his confident and upbeat nature; he sounded honest and sincere. Martin took a deep breath before speaking. 'I want a mirror, I want to see my face.'

Alan's voice dropped slightly. 'Well, I am sure you know that you have every right to a mirror but it has to be said that it's a little early for that. I would suggest that you give it at least a couple of days. Sometimes it helps to prepare yourself, to get used to the idea.'

'I . . . want . . . a . . . mirror . . . now,' Martin said slowly and precisely.

'Are you sure you don't want to wait until your parents are here?'

'No, I just told you, I . . . want . . . a mirror . . . now.'

'Have you ever seen someone with facial burns?'

'No.'

'Have you ever seen anyone who has been badly burnt anywhere on their body?'

'No, only in films.'

'We all know that the film world and the real world are two different worlds. I love films but they're just films. I need to warn you that when you look in the mirror you may be quite shocked by what you see. Whatever you see will be improved on in time. But Martin, you must know that you will always have some burns on your face. Your face will never be as it was. This may take some time for you to get used to. When you look in the mirror you are allowed to scream, cry or shout if you want to. Don't be afraid to express yourself – I look in the mirror and scream all the time!'

Even in this situation, Martin tried to smile. He felt himself smile inside but his face just couldn't. Martin understood what was being said to him but he still felt that he might just be locked in a nightmare. Although he had seen the damage that had been done to his legs, he knew that seeing his face would confirm that this was for real. He felt that he needed to pass that threshold. He was frightened but he didn't want to show his fear. 'I understand,' he muttered.

Alan stood up. 'Is there anything at all I can do for you now? Is there anything you need?'

'No, just a mirror.'

Alan had now lost his smile.

'Remember now, you can ask for me anytime and – if you don't like me – there are other counsellors and staff for you to choose from. I'll check out that mirror for you. Good luck, mate.'

For the next fifteen minutes Martin was left alone. He began to wonder if asking for the mirror was a wise thing to do. His body was beginning to ache, the various scratches and bruises had begun to make themselves known as the painkillers wore off, and

Martin's senses began to sharpen. He then had an idea which had not occurred to him before. He could sense the hardness of the skin on his face but he hadn't yet felt his face with his fingers. He thought about it, telling himself it would serve as a kind of preparation for what he was going to see but then he changed his mind. If he was to explore his face with his hands, too much would be left to the imagination. The best thing to do was to be brave and face his face head on.

Soon Nurse Ling and Alan Green re-entered the room. The nurse stood at the end of the bed holding something covered by a towel. Martin assumed that this was the mirror. Alan came closer down the side of the bed. Although not smiling, he still had that reassuring tone in his voice.

'Well, mate, here we are. I've just had a word with your parents. They are a bit concerned about you wanting a mirror in such a hurry but they did tell me that once you've made up your mind, nothing's going to stop you. They asked that I stay around, which is standard procedure anyway. So, here we go. Now, Martin, remember all that the doctor and I have told you.'

Nurse Ling unwrapped the mirror as if it were a precious object. She passed it to Alan making sure that the mirrored side was facing away from Martin so as not to allow him even a passing glance at his reflection. Martin watched their every move. When Alan had hold of the mirror he had a look at it as if to test it. Then he handed it to Martin, still making sure the mirrored side was pointing down.

'There you go. Sometimes it's best to have a glance, look away and then have a longer look. It's up to you, you're in control.'

For a moment Martin held the mirror against his chest, then he slowly lifted it up until he was looking into his own eyes. He suffered a silent shock. His eyes were completely red with only minute bits of white coming through. He focused on his pupils, leaving the rest of his face temporarily out of focus. His pupils looked untouched, unmoved by the chaos around them. But even when out of focus, he could not help but see the rough unevenness of his skin. Then Martin focused his eyes on the skin on his face. It was bright red in places, and brown in others. He noticed pinky white bits, which looked like flesh with no skin cover, where he could see veins. His whole face had swollen and changed shape. His right cheek was blistered, his left cheek had swollen – the two halves of his face looked completely different from each other. The contours of his face were jagged. On seeing his lips, which were swollen as if he had been in a fight, his breath left him for a moment. He instinctively shut his eyes, then slowly opened them again. He lifted a hand up to feel his head. Much of the back and sides of his hair had survived but the top front had mostly gone, only small patches were left. Martin was scared by what he saw but he could not look away.

Every few seconds different thoughts came into his head. *Is that really me? Why me? Maybe it will fall off and my real face will be underneath.* He began to really stare at his right cheek, checking every millimetre of it. *It looks like a mountain*, he thought. It was a strange thought but it was the first thing that came into his head. In a flash he remembered flying to Spain for a holiday and looking out at a mountain range with its valleys, its highs, and its lows. Martin saw his face as a miniature version of that wilderness. He put the mirror down on his lap and closed his eyes. Now he started to feel anger. His mind flashed back to Saturday night, not to the crash but to the moment just before he got into the car. He was seeing Pete Mosley's evil smile and hearing his voice saying, 'Come on, let's go riding,' and 'Have wheels will travel,' and most painfully, 'All right, ya gotta go to bed, we'll just take ya home.' That was the line that had tricked Martin into the car. He heard the lines over and over again in his head.

He opened his eyes, looking at the mirror once more, but this time he spoke as he stared. 'So this is me?'

Alan replied, 'It's you now but as you've heard, improvements can be made.'

Martin handed Alan the mirror and simply closed

his eyes. It was a clear signal to Alan and the nurse to leave. Martin listened to them go and kept his eyes shut. Now the image of his face was fixed in his mind. Then he opened his eyes and as he did so he began to cry uncontrollably. It was as if he had opened an emotional tap. He cried for his old face. He cried for his parents. He cried for Natalie. He cried for Matthew and Mark. He cried for his stupidity. Then he cried for his new face. He cried so much that his stomach hurt, he was out of breath and his eyes hurt. He could feel the tears leaving his eyes but he could not feel them running down his cheeks. He put his head under the sheets and cried himself to sleep. For the first time in his life, Martin cried and made no attempt to stop himself.

CHAPTER 8

~ The Other Pain ~

The next day Martin slept late. It was eleven o'clock when he woke up. The anaesthetic, painkillers and the various other drugs he had been given still affected him. Even though he was moving, he didn't feel fully awake.

Martin looked around the room. It had been transformed. It was obvious that his parents had been in earlier. Get well cards hung off string on the walls. On the table there was a photo of his parents, a photo of Natalie and his Walkman cassette player, complete with tapes and headphones. As he looked at the headphones, wondering how he could possibly use them, Dr Owens entered the room with his mother and father following her.

The doctor was the first to speak. 'Hello, Martin.'

'I'm awake again,' Martin said as his parents went to one side of the bed and the doctor to the other. 'I'm not sure how I'm going to get those headphones around my head though.'

His mother smiled. 'Well, your sense of humour is fine.'

Dr Owens went on to explain to Martin that some surgery would be recommended for cosmetic reasons, but that she thought it was best to let the skin heal as much as it could before then.

'From now on,' she said, 'nature should do the best it can.'

She then pulled over a chair and sat down looking at Martin with a matter of fact look on her face. 'Martin, I have just explained to your parents that the skin on your face will never be as it was before. I expect your legs and hands to heal up soon, but you will have to be patient with your face.'

Martin turned to look at his parents. His mother was struggling to hold back the tears, and her voice trembled as she spoke. 'We love you, son. We'll do all we can for you, you know it.'

Dr Owens took a deep breath and continued, 'I understand that you have known Mark Thorpe for a long time.'

'Yes,' Martin replied. 'Where is he? How bad is he?'

'He was released from this hospital today. He has two broken ribs and a fractured wrist. Now – Graham Fisher?'

'Who?'

'Graham Fisher.'

Martin's father interrupted, 'The driver of the car, son.'

'You mean Apache, I don't really know him.'

'Well, he was lucky. He got away with a few bruises, but he has been to court and I am informed that he is now in youth custody. And Peter Mosley?'

'Yeah, I know him,' Martin replied.

Dr Owens paused. 'How well?'

'I don't know him that well. He used to go the same school as me. He hangs around the Boleyn Estate.'

Dr Owens lowered her voice. 'I'm sorry to have to tell you this, Martin, but Peter Mosley died from his injuries after going through the front windscreen.'

Martin went silent. There was only a small part of him that mourned Pete's passing. He was a person he knew very little, a person who he had never had much respect for. What had stunned Martin into silence was the realisation of how close *he* had been to death. He looked at his parents and for the first time in his life, he really wanted to hold them and tell them how much he loved them. He looked at his surroundings. He looked at his hands. He was grateful for his existence, but he couldn't find words to express how he felt.

Turning back to his parents, he asked, 'Pete's mom and dad, do they know?'

'Do you know his mom and dad, son?' his father asked.

'No.'

'No one does, son.'

'But Dad, he must have a mom and dad some-where.'

'No one knows, son, don't let it worry you.'

Soon Martin's parents and Dr Owens left, leaving Martin to take in the news he had just received. He spent the next two hours sitting silently listening to his breathing and his heartbeat. The pain mattered very little now. Now he saw himself as lucky, lucky to be alive. He had very little love for Pete Mosley but he could not get his face out of his mind now. *And what about Peter's parents*, he thought. *He must have parents, someone must love him.* Again Martin began to think at a frantic pace. *I should never have gone to that club . . . we should have never went through that estate . . . I should never have got in that car . . . I should have known it was stolen. It's all my fault, I persuaded Mark to get into that car.* Martin thought so much that he got a headache, and in his upright position he hung his head and began to fall asleep. Even as he was falling asleep, he was still asking questions. *Why didn't I go with my instincts and not get in that car? . . . Why didn't I go with Matthew? . . . Why didn't I?*

'Martin, are you awake?'

The interruption seemed to echo around his head.

77

It was Dr Owens with somebody else, a man wearing a black leather jacket and jeans.

'Martin, can we talk to you?' the doctor continued.

'Yeah, OK.' Martin didn't mean it, he would have preferred to have been left alone, but he felt weak and he couldn't say no.

'Martin, this is Detective Inspector Byrd. He needs to speak to you about the accident. He won't be long. This is not an interrogation and I won't be leaving the room. Can you manage that?'

'Yes, I can.'

'OK.' Dr Owens went and stood by the door as if guarding the entrance and DI Byrd sat on the chair next to the bed.

'Now, Martin, I realise that you have been through a lot over the last few days. Soon I am going to have to take a statement from you but for now I just need a couple of answers – OK?'

'OK.'

'How well do you know Graham Fisher, or Apache as he was also known?'

'I don't know him. The night of the crash was when I met him.'

'Did you get on with him?'

'I hardly spoke to him, he's a nutter.'

'How do you know he was a nutter?'

'Just the way he was acting and driving – he wasn't listening to anyone.'

'Did he try and sell you anything?'

'No.'

'Did you see him throw anything out of the car?'

Martin paused. Dr Owens was watching silently, her eyes fixed on Martin. The detective could sense that he was on to something. His voice hardened and he pushed for more.

'Come on now, Martin, we know from your medical records that you had been drinking alcohol that night, but we haven't come here because of a little underage drinking. This is a bit more serious than that. Did you see Apache throw anything?'

'NO – NO – I didn't see Apache throw anything – I saw Pete throw something.'

'That's better. Where? Can you remember?'

'I think it was by the sports centre on Prince Regents Lane.'

'On the corner?'

'Yes.'

'What did you see him throw?'

'I don't know what it was, just a small bag of some kind.'

'OK, that's all I need. As I said, I am going to need a statement soon but you must realise that you may find yourself in trouble for accepting a lift in a stolen car. We'll talk about that at a later date. Take it easy for now.'

Dr Owens and DI Byrd both left. Once again,

Martin was alone. It seemed that life in hospital went from one extreme to the other. There were moments of intense activity with people all wanting to know, feel and look crammed into this small room, followed by moments of silence which quickly led on to sleep. DI Byrd's visit had taken his mind off his injuries temporarily, but now he had nothing to distract him.

He raised both his hands and for the first time he began to touch his face. He prodded to see how much pressure he could bear. It even *felt* like an unexplored wilderness with miniature mountains. Not one bit of his face was smooth. The outer skin was hard but he could feel the soft, swollen flesh underneath. Most of the sensations came though his fingertips. Considering the extent of his injuries, he was still surprised by the fact that his legs, although not burnt, hurt more than his face.

Martin also had other worries. How were his friends going to react to him? He had Natalie and Matthew on his mind. He needed to know more about what had happened to Mark and wondered what the police were going to do. He had decided that he would take the blame for Mark getting into trouble. He wondered if he would have to go to court, or worse still if he would end up in a young offenders' home.

CHAPTER 9

~ The Unprepared ~

For the next couple of days Martin had regular visits
from Dr Owens and his parents. His parents visited him twice a day. With every visit they brought more
gifts and personal possessions to decorate his room. He
now had a poster of West Ham football team taped to
his wall, and on his table he had a bowl of fruit, a stack
of comics and football annuals. Moving slowly, he was
now getting out of bed and walking around his tiny
room, but he would never venture out into the ward;
he wasn't ready to meet strangers. Martin had also
started to take solid food and as the swelling of his lips
reduced, he began to speak more fluently.

Dr Owens was happy with Martin's progress, and
she told him that it would soon be time for a cosmetic
operation, a skin graft. Martin tried to tell himself
that, despite all that had happened, he was still the
same person he had been before, but deep down he
knew it was going to be hard. He now realised that
being an extrovert took a lot of energy.

The two nurses and Martin were a little more relaxed with each other now. Martin now knew the male nurse's name was Dylan Davis and that he supported Newcastle United. Nurse Ling had been born in the very hospital she was now working in. She did her training in Central London and went straight to Newham Parkside, where she had wanted to work ever since she had been at school. He had spent quite a lot of time talking to Nurse Ling. She couldn't understand why he would want a picture of a football team on his wall and he was just beginning to understand why she only ever spoke of two role models in her life. The only role models she had were her mother and father who had both come to England penniless. They had taught themselves to speak English and made sure that she received the best education possible.

One morning Nurse Ling explained to Martin that the time had come for him to have his first bath.

'It will hurt a little the first time, but that's why me and Nurse Davis are here.'

Martin hid his nervousness. 'OK, where do we do it?'

'Right here,' Nurse Ling replied. 'You won't even have to leave your bed.'

The nurses left the room and returned twenty minutes later manoeuvring a trolley into the room. The trolley had various bottles and towels on the bottom shelf but on the top shelf and most noticeable was a large silver bowl and a large silver jug. Nurse Ling began to pour from the jug into the bowl whilst Nurse Davis told Martin what was happening.

'In the bowl there is lukewarm water and Nurse Ling is adding a saline solution to it. Saline helps to reduce the risk of infection. What we are going to do next is to wet these towels and gently pad them on to your skin. It will sting a little at first but you will soon get used to it.'

'Don't worry,' Nurse Ling interjected, 'it sounds worse than it is.'

'Yes, she's right,' Nurse Davis continued. 'Just lie back and think of West Ham and it will be over before you get to half-time.'

Martin eased his pyjamas off. He was then instructed to lie on his back so that he could see the first applications of the towels and not be fearful or taken by surprise. Martin felt highly embarrassed by this – he hated being naked in front of the nurses, but his most overwhelming emotion was one of helplessness. He hated not doing things for himself and he hated lying back and waiting for something to happen to him. He definitely couldn't think of West Ham.

Nurse Ling dipped the small towels into the bowl, squeezed off the excess liquid and dabbed Martin's skin lightly. She dipped each towel only once and dabbed with the greatest care. Martin felt a mild burning sensation when the towel first touched his skin but then it cooled quickly. After being cleaned from his toes right up to his neck, Martin turned over to lie face down. Nurse Davis placed a sterilised towel on the pillow and gently eased Martin's face on to it. Then his back received the same careful treatment. When the whole of his body was done, Nurse Ling gave the same treatment to his face. But now she was most careful. Every touch was gentle, so gentle that Martin hardly felt a thing. Just a light tingly sensation that came after the applications. The whole process took half an hour.

When the nurses had left and Martin was in his pyjamas again and back in bed, he began once more to reflect on his situation. The bathing wasn't as painful as he had thought it would be, but his body did feel as if it had undergone a change. He turned his head to the left as far as it would go, and then to the right. He bent his head down as far as it would go and then up and back as far as it would go. He put his left hand in front of his face and slowly made a fist. As his finger tips pushed against his palm, it felt as if the tender skin would crack. Although he didn't have the strength to form a firm fist, he was pleased that he could at least now make a weak one. He then repeated the action with his right hand.

There was a knock on the door. Martin quickly put his hands down. No one had knocked on the door before. His first thought was that the police had come for the real questioning. He said nothing. The door handle turned slowly and to his surprise Natalie's face appeared at the edge of the door. 'Hello, can we come in?' She seemed nervous.

'Yeah, come in. Who's we?'

Natalie entered, followed by Mark and then Matthew. 'It's me' . . . 'And me.'

Martin sprang to life. There was much to talk about and he was glad to be speaking to people of his own age, better still his best friends. But the atmosphere was tense. It was his friends: they were nervous. Natalie perched on the edge of the bed, and the two boys took the seats.

'So, how's the outside world?' Martin enquired.

'The same,' Matthew replied. 'How come you ain't got a telly?'

'I dunno, I haven't really thought about television.'

'And radio?' Natalie asked.

'I haven't listened to radio either. Have you ever listened to hospital radio? It's bad for your health.'

They all laughed at Martin's joke. Then there was an uncomfortable pause.

'So, you don't even know what's happened to West Ham?' Natalie asked.

'No. What's happened?'

'Nothing,' she smiled, 'they haven't played.'

Martin noticed that none of the three had looked him in the face while he was looking at them, but the moment his eyes were off them, he could feel them staring. The talk was trivial until Mark brought up the subject of the press. 'Have you seen the Newham Echo?'

'No.'

'We're in it, guy, and it don't look good.'

'What does it say? Martin asked.

'It says stuff about the crash,' Mark replied. 'It says DRUG DEALER KILLED IN CAR CRASH. It named us, made me and you sound like druggies.'

'I don't want to say this but I got to,' Matthew interrupted. 'I told you, I said you were mad to get in that car.'

Voices started to be raised until Natalie calmed everyone down. 'Look, newspapers always make things sound bad. Have you got any good music?' Natalie looked towards the Walkman as she asked.

'I haven't really listened to any,' Martin replied, 'but I'm sure it's just my old stuff. Do me a favour and bring me some rap music in.'

Natalie smiled. 'No problem.'

They had now been in the room for nearly half an hour and no one had said anything about Martin's face until Martin himself asked Mark about his injuries. 'So, what happened to you, then?'

Mark lifted up his shirt to show that his lower torso was wrapped in a large bandage and his right wrist was bandaged. 'A couple of broken ribs and a fractured wrist – I was in the Henniker Ward for a couple of days. What about you, guy?'

'Well, what can I say? No broken bones, no fractures, a few cuts and bruises on my body and I am still here. I'm sorry, Mark, man, it was my fault. I shouldn't have told you to get into that car.'

'Forget it, man, things happen. How were you to know things would end up like this?'

'But I should have been able to see that those two were nutters and that that car was nicked. It's my fault.' Martin held his head down as he spoke.

Silence fell in the room. No one knew how to respond. Matthew felt he had to. 'It's no one's fault. Are you in a lot of pain?'

'Yeah but I got used to it now. It feels pretty normal after a while.'

'Do you know when you'll be out?' Mark asked.

'No, but I know I'll be out – soon.'

Martin desperately wanted to ask his friends about his face. But he didn't want to sound too serious.

'Do you think you could handle a friend as ugly as me?'

There was another uncomfortable silence before Natalie spoke.

'Don't say that, Martin, you'll soon be better.'

'I won't get much better,' Martin replied. 'So,' he continued, looking at Matthew, 'is there such a thing as the Gang of Three without me?'

Matthew replied quietly, 'As far as I'm concerned, you're still my mate.'

Mark quickly changed the conversation and began to ask Martin how the hospital staff were treating him. But the conversation seemed staged and artificial, and soon it was time for visitors to go. Almost as if planned, Mark and Matthew left, leaving Natalie alone with Martin. Natalie stood close to Martin. Martin held his hand out to her. She looked at it before gently taking hold of it. She felt the rough jagged skin of his hand and he felt the smooth, silk-like texture of hers. For a moment they looked at each other in silence. Martin's eyes were fixed upon Natalie's but Natalie found it difficult: her eyes shifted to the left, then onto Martin, then to the right, then back onto Martin.

'Ain't you going to give us a kiss then?' Martin asked.

Natalie stood expressionless. She didn't speak, and Martin could see that she had no idea how to reply.

'I'm only joking,' Martin said, letting go of her hand.

'I'd better go now,' Natalie said. 'I'll get you some rap tapes tomorrow.' And she went.

Martin was left not knowing what to think. These were his closest friends and they had found it so difficult facing him. He felt a kind of anger towards them but then he thought of how he would have reacted if he had been in their position. He convinced himself that he would have reacted much better. He also tried to convince himself that he would have kissed Natalie if the roles were reversed but in truth he wasn't sure. Then, without warning, more negative thoughts flooded into his mind. *Maybe I deserve this. Maybe this is a punishment from God. Maybe I should have believed in God more. Maybe no one will like me.* Thoughts like this tormented him until they became like another voice in his head. *I shouldn't be the leader of the gang, I have brought pain and unhappiness to my friends and my parents. Maybe I should have died.* He began to shake, he felt like running anywhere to escape himself. At the point when the voice seemed so loud that he felt his head was going to burst, he pressed the red emergency button by his bed. A nurse he didn't know ran into the room.

'What's the matter? she said.

'I want to see Alan, the Scottish man, the counsellor,' Martin said, speaking quickly. 'And I want a mirror.'

'I'm sorry,' she said. 'I'm not sure if I can give you a mirror without authorisation. Let me get Mr Green.'

The nurse left the room walking as fast as she could without running.

When she returned, she was panting as if she had run miles. 'Mr Green will be with you in five minutes, OK?'

'OK,' Martin replied. 'I'm all right now. I just want to be left alone until he comes.'

'Are you sure you're all right?' said the nurse.

'Yes, I'm all right,' Martin shouted. 'I just wanna see Alan and I just wanna see me.'

The nurse left.

In less than five minutes Alan arrived. He still seemed to be wearing a smile. 'What can I do for you, mate?' he said sitting at Martin's bedside.

Martin replied, 'I'm just fed up, man. I just had a visit from my best friends and my girlfriend and they all acted like they hardly knew me.'

Alan's voice became lower but the smile was still there. 'This is to be expected, Martin. The first thing you have to do is to come to terms with the way you are. Once you've done that you have solved many of your problems. As far as your friends are concerned, well, they have to figure out their own problems. They have to come to terms with themselves. They also have to think about how they see you, and sometimes, Martin, you may find that you will have to help them. They don't mean to be nasty, they just don't know how to deal with the situation.'

Martin reached out to take the mirror that Alan was holding in his hand. 'Can I keep this mirror in here?' Martin asked.

'Are you sure you want to? It may not be such a good idea.'

Martin raised his voice slightly, his tone assertive. 'I want to, I know what I want. You said I've got to come to terms with the way I look, so I am. I want to see me, and I want to see me when I like, OK?'

Passing Martin the mirror Alan said quietly, 'All right, just don't torture yourself. You're still the same guy. And remember that I am one member of staff you can get any time. The nurses can even ring me at home, so use me if you need me.'

Martin felt much better after the conversation with Alan. He realised that nothing was solved, but he needed to sound off to someone and that was what Alan was there for. Soon Alan was saying goodbye, leaving Martin to sleep with the mirror leaning against the fruit bowl. Martin had decided that he wanted to see himself when he woke up.

CHAPTER 10

~ To Do or Not to Do ~

Every day for the next week Martin woke up looking at himself. It was an unusual way of doing things. For a while it worried Alan and his parents but Martin would not let the mirror leave his room. He watched every inch of his face as it healed. He noted that it didn't take very long for the bruises on his legs to disappear. He was fascinated by the stitches on the two larger cuts. He dreaded the day when they would have to be removed but when he asked when that would be, he was told that the stitches would simply dissolve, and so they did. Every day bits of stitching just disappeared until there was nothing left.

Martin began to move around his small room. He was determined to be independent, and that meant being able to wash himself. And being able to wash himself meant walking out of his room and through the ward to the shower. For his first venture out he chose a Sunday morning when the ward was at its quietest. With his towel in hand he stood by the door taking deep breaths. He opened the door slowly, stepped through and turned back to close it. Then he turned to see the ward. Most people were asleep, some were reading newspapers and a couple just seemed to be looking and thinking. Those who looked at Martin just looked away. Martin was relieved. *Of course*, he thought, *why should they find me so odd, they are all burns victims themselves, I am on a Burns Unit.* Now it was him doing all the staring. As he walked down the ward he began to look at other people's injuries. A few people didn't look like they had injuries at all but Martin knew that these people probably had burns on their bodies. For Martin this was a liberating moment. Anyone who noticed Martin didn't give him a second look and by the time he'd reached the end of the ward he wanted to walk back just for the fun of it. Soon Martin was showering or going for walks on the ward anytime he felt like it. Being seen by other people got easier each time.

Martin's parents still visited him every day and every couple of days Natalie, Matthew and Mark would visit. The visits by his friends were the most difficult. Matthew and Mark always had very little to say; they never spoke about the events surrounding the crash now unless they were quoting newspapers. Although Natalie was polite and helpful, Martin spent very little time alone with her.

As the days went by Martin began to feel more at home in his room. The football posters and creature comforts had helped and he was beginning to develop a real appreciation of rap music. Natalie brought him new tapes with every visit and Martin's headphones were now usually found on his head. The front of his hair was beginning to grow back and with the help of the hospital's visiting barber, he had the rest of his hair cut short so that the new growth would not be so obvious. His face was not really healing but settling down. The extremely red parts and the extremely white parts were trying to find their natural colour but the damage to the contours of his face stayed the same. One of his mother's main concerns had gone: he was now eating anything that was put in front of him.

On the morning of Martin's sixteenth day in hospital Dr Owens and Nurse Ling entered the room just as he was finishing his breakfast. Martin had picked up a new skill. He knew the hospital staff so well that he could tell what mode they were in by the looks on their faces and the way they entered the room. He could tell routine visits from progress reports, or *how are you doing* visits from *we need to talk* visits. He could see this was a *we need to talk* visit. Dr Owens sat on the seat in front of Martin. Martin sat up in his bed.

'Hello.'

'Hello, Martin,' Dr Owens replied. 'How are you today?'

'I'm OK, Doctor.'

'Martin, I need to talk to you about where we go from here. As you can see, the injuries to your face are not disappearing but you are feeling less discomfort now, aren't you?'

'Yes.'

'The swelling around your lips and eyes has gone down considerably and you are beginning to have more control over your facial muscles now.'

'That's right.' Martin knew what was coming.

'Well, I think it's time for us to consider a bit of physical reconstruction, or plastic surgery.'

'Will you really use plastic?'

'No, we never really use plastic and anyway in your case physical reconstruction is probably too strong a term. Because you have no problems with your bones, all I shall be trying to do is to give your face a smoother look. I think we can get rid of some of those rough edges. Now let me tell you how I plan to do this. I want to use an autograft – that means a skin graft taken from another part of your body and grafted on to your face.'

'Hang on a minute,' Martin interjected. 'Where will the skin come from?'

'Well, I suggest we take some off one of your thighs. The skin at the top of your thighs is perfectly all right and I only need a small amount. I need to do two grafts, one on your right cheek and one on your forehead.'

Martin was listening carefully to everything she had to say. He knew how important this was and he wanted to make sure he understood everything. 'Will you be doing this operation, then, or someone else?' he asked.

'I'll be doing it. I'll have my team of course but I'll be doing the actual surgery. Now, Martin, you can say no – after all, this is basically a cosmetic operation. You can decide to do without any surgery at all, because this is about you. You have the ultimate decision what to do or not to do and only you can truly decide what is a presentable face for you.'

There was a long silence before Martin uttered, 'Heavy, man.'

Dr Owens stood up. 'I will be speaking with your parents soon, so think things over and I'll talk to you later. It may sound heavy but it's just that I want you to take as much control as you can. You are the boss.'

Nurse Ling removed Martin's food trolley and they both left the room, leaving Martin alone with his thoughts once more. Martin spent that morning in silence, thinking about what was to come and periodically looking at himself in the mirror. Time passed and at around midday Dr Owens and both his parents entered the room. His father was carrying a bowl full of grapes, peaches and bananas and his mother carried a vase of flowers.

'Hello, Mom, hello, Dad. Put the fruit on the table and I'll eat the flowers now.'

His mother smiled, the doctor raised an eyebrow as if only slightly amused and his father said, 'That's very funny, son,' as he put the fruit on the table which was now beginning to look like a fruit stall at a market. His mother passed him the flowers and he barely managed to find space for them on the table.

'So what about the operation, son?' his father asked. 'We think it's best, how about you, son?'

Martin paused for a moment. 'What can go wrong?'

'The only thing that I'm worried about is infection. There is a slight risk but because it's your own skin, the chances of that are extremely low,' said Dr Owens.

Martin picked up the mirror and looked at himself as he spoke. 'When would you do the operation?'

'I can do it any time,' Dr Owens replied, 'but you should have a day or so to get used to the idea.'

'Will there be a big difference in the way I look?'

'Well, it's hard to say,' Dr Owens said while looking into Martin's face. 'The colour of your skin will even out and you should lose some of the roughness, but we can never tell how big the difference will be. There will be an improvement, though.'

'OK,' Martin said, 'let's do it.'

There was a sigh of relief from his parents and the

doctor began to explain the procedure to Martin. Skin was to be taken from his right thigh. He would be given a general anaesthetic which would mean that he wouldn't see or feel a thing until after the operation. Dr Owens also explained that in her opinion he didn't need too much skin grafting and that maybe one operation would do. She told Martin that some people just keep having more and more plastic surgery in the hope that they will end up with what they think others think is a normal face. She thought this was an unhealthy attitude.

'Whatever you decide,' she said, 'this will be a testing time for you.'

CHAPTER 11

~ Patient B503 ~

Two days later, on the day of his operation, Martin woke early and decided to go for a walk on the ward. Unable to have breakfast before the operation, he walked around watching others having theirs. He was now playing a before and after game in his mind. He was trying to look at the other patients without staring and guessing whether those with facial injuries had had operations. Everybody became a before, an after or a don't know. He felt guilty doing this but he wanted to see what could be done by surgery. As he stood looking down the ward, Martin heard a quiet voice from behind him.

'All right.'

Martin turned to see a boy about his age standing in front of him, with a face so disfigured that he gasped with surprise.

'Wow – I'm sorry,' Martin's awkwardness was obvious and he could not stop staring at the boy's face.

'It's all right,' the boy replied, 'I'm used to it. Are

you Martin?'

'Yes – how do you know my name?' Martin's eyes wandered around the boy's face. He now realised how his friends must have felt when they first saw him.

'Miss Ling told me about you, said you were a West Ham supporter.'

'Yeah, I am, are you?'

'I'm not really a supporter, I've never seen them play, only on telly, but I like them. So what happened to you?'

This took Martin by complete surprise. It was the first time he had ever been asked the question and he was being asked by someone who he saw as worse off than himself. Martin didn't know how much to tell. He wondered if he should just say he'd been in a fire, or just in a crash, or should he say how he got in the crash. In the end he said, 'I was in a car crash – the car caught fire.'

'Gosh,' the boy replied. 'How long have you been here?'

'Just over two weeks – I'm having an operation today. How long have you been here?'

'Well . . . I was born like this . . . well, not like this . . . but I was born with severe facial disfigurements. I've been in here six times and I've had eight operations. I could stay on one of the other wards if I wanted to but I like staying on this one. All the nurses here know me and I like them. They're cool. I had an operation a couple of days ago and I'm going home today.'

Martin couldn't believe what he was hearing. He admired this boy's confidence. 'What's your name?'

'Anthony. Where's your room?'

'Down there,' Martin pointed. 'Do you wanna see it?'

'Yeah.'

As they walked down to Martin's room, Anthony greeted most of the people in the ward, or they shouted hello to him. He seemed to know nearly everybody and Martin could see that he was well liked. Martin showed Anthony his many football books. Through the headphones he introduced him to his favourite rap tunes, and he ended up by showing him photos of his mom and dad. Amongst the photos was a picture of himself with Natalie.

'Is that your sister?' Anthony asked.

'No, man, that's my girl.'

'What, your girlfriend?'

'Yeah, man.'

'What's her name?'

'Natalie.'

'She's not bad, guy. Is she sticking by you?'

'What do you mean?' Martin asked, puzzled.

'Is she still going to hang out with you when you get out? Some girls don't, you know. Some girls say "Let's just be friends" and things like that.'

Martin was caught off guard. He wasn't sure how to answer. 'Yeah, man, she's sticking by me all right, she was here yesterday.'

'Shame.'

'What's a shame?' Martin asked.

'It's a shame I didn't see her,' Anthony replied as he winked.

They both laughed and slapped hands. Then Anthony looked at his watch and headed for the door. 'I gotta go, guy, my mom will be here soon. Don't worry about your operation, man, you'll be OK, they're good here. I'll see you around. Say hello to Natalie for me.'

Martin was on a high. Anthony had really cheered him up. The way Anthony talked about himself with ease inspired him and there was much about him that reminded Martin of how he used to be. Martin realised that although Anthony's face had shocked him at first, he'd soon forgotten about his face and become more interested in his character and showing him around. Martin climbed into bed smiling.

Martin had just put on his theatre gown when Nurse Ling and two men in white coats came in pushing a theatre trolley. Nurse Ling asked Martin to lie down on the theatre trolley, which he did in nervous silence, and they were off. He lay on his back watching the ceiling above him. He knew where he was as he went down the ward but when he left the ward it was new territory. All he could see were ceilings and lights; every so often they would go through rubber doors. When he looked to his left he saw white coats, when he looked to the right he saw white coats. But although he couldn't see her, Nurse Ling's voice comforted him. 'It won't be long now, Martin,' and 'Not far to go now.' Then the busy, draughty corridors were replaced by the calm warmth of the operating theatre.

'Here we are now, Martin,' Nurse Ling announced.

Martin could hear people talking about him. He was being referred to as patient B503. Nurse Ling stayed by him. 'We're just double checking that you are who you say you are.'

'I am not a number, I am a free man,' Martin said half jokingly.

'Good morning, Martin.' It was Dr Owens leaning over him. She was now all dressed in white as far as Martin could see and looking very much in control. 'This is Mr Carr, he's our anaesthetist today. He's going to help you relax.'

Mr Carr took Martin's arm and started to wipe a spot with wet cotton wool.

'Now you haven't eaten anything today, have you, Martin?' His voice was well lived in and serious.

'No,' Martin replied.

'You're just going to feel a small prick as the needle enters.'

Martin felt it.

'And now, Martin, will you count to ten for me.'

'One, two, three . . . , four . . . , five . . . '

Martin opened his eyes slowly. He recognised the ceiling. He was back in his room. It felt like five minutes later, but in fact it was six hours later. The operation had taken three hours and it was now 5 o'clock. He lay still. His face felt as if it had been pulled and stretched in places; in other places it felt tight. He could feel that hands had been all over his face. His throat was dry and he felt very hungry. He began to check his limbs for feeling. Everything was coming to life, it all felt OK. He lay still for about fifteen minutes before he manoeuvred himself into his sitting position. Then he looked to the table for his mirror but it wasn't there. He rang his bell and nurses came running but he was told that he would only be given a mirror when he had seen the doctor. He had neither the strength nor the will to protest.

The doctor and Nurse Ling came soon afterwards. Dr Owens looked towards Martin and smiled. 'Well, Martin, from a surgeon's point of view the operation went well. I'm sorry about having to remove your mirror but it's standard procedure.'

As the doctor was speaking, Nurse Ling left the room and quickly returned with the mirror in her hand. Dr Owens continued. 'Your face will look and feel more bruised than it was before you went into theatre but it will soon calm down.'

Nurse Ling handed Martin the mirror. He put it on his lap, and then the doctor and nurse left the room.

As soon as Martin was alone he looked into the mirror. The doctor was right: it did look worse than before surgery. Although he had been warned not to expect miracles, he had still believed that he would look much better. He could see the outline of the grafted skin and that the grafted skin was clearly a different colour from the original skin. His face felt tight. He raised his eyebrows but instead of the usual lines, the whole area of new skin moved upwards. Martin slammed the mirror down on his bed before reaching over to the table to turn on his personal stereo. His breathing quickened with anger. He put on his headphones and listened to music until he fell asleep.

Later that evening Martin had a visit from his parents. There was a little talk of how the operation had went. His father said very little as usual and his mother was being her kind, caring self. After forcing yet more fruit onto the table and removing the fruit which was now decomposing, she attended unnecessarily to Martin's bedclothes, smoothing out and tucking in bits of the sheets and blankets.

As she folded the bed covers under Martin's arms, she burst into tears, crying loudly. 'Oh my God. What's happened to my son? What have I done, God? What's happening to us?'

Her voice was loud. It went outside the room and down the ward. She flopped over Martin's bed like a mourner over a coffin, weak and out of control.

'My beautiful son, my beautiful son. Why did it happen to my son, why?'

She cried and cried. Martin's father put his hand on her shoulder. 'Come on, Wendy, calm down. We ain't done nothing wrong.'

Just then Alan Green entered the room. 'Now Mrs Turner, let's have you sitting down,' he said, taking her by the hand and guiding her to the seat.

She continued to cry but as the minutes passed, she began to take control of herself. Alan Green soothed her with his words, and then, as he left, he put a thumb up to Martin. Soon his mother was apologising to him for her outburst.

'I'm sorry, son.'

'Don't be sorry, Mom.'

'I'm showing you up.'

'What, showing me up in front of Dad?'

There was laughter as Martin went on to recall times when she had really shown him up.

After Martin's parents had left, Alan Green came back to see Martin. He wanted to make sure that

Martin was not too affected by what had happened.

'How are you feeling?'

'I'm OK, I think.'

'Why, are you not sure?'

'I feel kinda OK but I'm wondering if my mom knows something I don't know.'

'No,' Alan said smiling. 'A lot of parents act like that. Your mother also has to get used to the idea.'

'But she was getting all religious and stuff, you saw her. I ain't never seen her like that before,' Martin said.

'It's probably because she thought that the operation would put things better straight away.'

'Yeah, I got a bit of a shock when I looked in the mirror myself,' Martin admitted.

'The way the face looks immediately after grafting is not the way it stays. Newly grafted skin needs time to take – as we call it. She just needed to cry and that's very normal.'

Martin needed these words of comfort.

CHAPTER 12

~ What the Officer Said ~

Five days after the operation, and twenty-three days after being admitted to hospital, Martin was ready to be discharged from Newham Parkside. His thigh had begun to grow new skin and his face had improved. There were no infection problems after the operation and the two newly grafted pieces of skin had begun to settle in. The burns on his hands had now healed as much as they could, the minor cuts and scratches that he had received in the crash had all gone. There wasn't any more that the hospital could do for him for a while. Once again it was time to let nature do its thing. Martin's legs felt weak. He hadn't run or gone for a long walk for over three weeks. Martin had a daydream about doing gymnastics, going for long walks and playing football whilst in hospital. After listening to so much music, he longed for the day to come when he could dance. But he also knew that gymnastics, football, dancing and even walking were never going to be the same again with his new face.

Martin's parents arrived early to help him pack. The daily presents they had been bringing in, added to his friends' gifts, meant that there was quite a lot of packing to do. His mother had brought him a brand new designer outfit with a pocket specially made for a Walkman and other pockets specially made for spare tapes. Martin put the outfit on straight away and immediately made use of the pockets. It was an extra baggy, brown, two-piece outfit that his mother described as cut curtains. But Martin had seen a similar outfit being worn by the rapper MC Kitty Kat on the front of a music cassette and had said he wanted something like it. Fortunately for Martin, his mother would buy almost anything to make him happy.

As they packed, Alan Green popped in to say goodbye. He gave Martin a card with his home and hospital phone numbers on it and told them all that they were free to contact him at any time. Then he bid them farewell and continued on his rounds.

'Come on,' said Martin's father. 'We'll get a taxi at the hospital reception.'

Martin had never walked off the Burns Unit before. As he left the ward, other patients said goodbye or waved. Many of them had never spoken to Martin but they had got used to seeing him on the ward. As he walked to reception, Martin saw a whole world of people. Some were patients, some were staff and some were visitors, and for the first time Martin thought he was being stared at publicly.

Getting into the taxi was a relief. It was like escaping but the summer sun was shining brightly and hurting his eyes. He had seen very little natural sunlight and the summer heat was something that oppressed him after three weeks in an air conditioned state. He was aware of every turn the taxi made. His ears were acutely aware of all the sounds of the street but all he did was to stare at the seat in front of him. Not once did Martin look out of the taxi window into the street until they arrived home and even then he only gave his home a quick glance before rushing in, leaving his parents to carry all his bags.

Martin spent the rest of the day unpacking and rearranging his room. He was pleased to be home and back in his room. Although he knew he was privileged to have had his own room at the hospital, he had missed his own space.

Before going to sleep that night, Martin had a long hard look at himself in the mirror. It was different now. Looking like he did at home was somehow different from looking like he did in the Burns Unit. He was now in familiar surroundings with an unfamiliar face.

The next morning after breakfast, Martin, dressed in his West Ham football kit, was riding his mother's exercise bike when the doorbell rang. He stopped for a moment as he let the unfamiliar sound of the doorbell die out and then he continued to pedal.

Downstairs he could hear the mumblings of a conversation but he paid it no attention until he heard his name being called.

'Martin, Martin, can you come down, love,' his mother called. 'There's someone here to see you.'

It was DI Byrd with a colleague. 'I'm sorry for coming to see you so soon after you've been discharged from the hospital but I do need to speak to you,' said DI Byrd.

He looked very formal but spoke very casually. 'My superiors think I should be working harder.'

'Sit down, mate,' his father interrupted, pointing to a chair.

When they were all seated, DI Byrd continued.

'Now, Martin, yesterday I had a talk with your friend Mark Thorpe. I have a signed statement from him telling the story of the accident from his point of view. What I need now is your story. If you tell me what happened from when you left the club until the accident happened, my colleague Detective Hudson will do the writing. You and your parents can check it and, if you're happy, all you have to do is sign it and we can move on to the next stage.'

'OK,' Martin replied. He wasn't looking forward to this. On various occasions he had had small flashbacks but up until now he had not had to go through the whole thing in one sitting. He hadn't been expecting this.

He did his best to relay what had happened that night. His parents, who were hearing the whole story for the first time, just sat and listened. Detective Hudson wrote away and DI Byrd had very little prompting to do as Martin let the story pour out, trying hard not to omit a single thing. When all was done, DI Byrd had to pick up on one point.

'I have to ask you this straight out, Martin. I've asked you before and now you're making your statement, I have to ask you again. It's important, so don't let your parents, don't let your friends, don't even let your enemies, put you off telling the truth. Did Apache or Peter Mosley offer you any drugs?'

'No,' Martin replied agitated. 'I told you already, no. What's the matter? Don't you believe me?'

'I believe you, mate, but I've been asked to make sure. You see we know they were stealing and dealing in drugs, and we know they had been dealing on the night of the crash but we can't find no evidence.'

'Well, we had no drugs from them. Like I said in the hospital, I did see Pete throw something out of the car but I don't know what it was.'

Detective Hudson read the statement out to the family and Martin signed it with his father as witness. Two hours had passed and DI Byrd had not finished yet.

'At this point, Martin, I have to officially caution you.'

'For what?'

'For accepting a lift in a stolen car.'

'I didn't know it was stolen. I didn't steal it.'

'Calm down, Martin,' his mother said firmly. 'Listen to what the officer has to say.'

DI Byrd continued. 'You must understand, I have to do things by the book. As you said in your own words, they were joy-riding in the car before you got in it. A formal caution is just a warning to you that if it ever happens again you must ask who the car belongs to, if you're not sure, don't get in. Anyone who reads my report will see that basically you're a victim of circumstance but you must realise how close you and Mark came to death. Peter Mosley was bad news, Graham Fisher still is bad news. This caution is just a warning – stay away from scum like that.'

Martin had got the message. He nodded a yes. DI Byrd dropped his tone. 'Peter Mosley was buried last week in a council grave. No one knows where his mother is and after he was buried, we traced his father to a prison up north where he's doing a life sentence. Graham Fisher or Apache is going to jail.' His voice softened even more. 'His parents love him, he just doesn't love himself. He's been in and out since he was thirteen.'

Then DI Byrd handed Martin another sheet of paper. 'Sign there, please, it just confirms the fact that you've been cautioned.'

Martin signed the caution and again his father

signed as witness. As the police officers left, DI Byrd told them that he hoped never to see them again in the line of duty. When the door was closed, Martin, his mother and his father hugged, all three together in the hallway.

CHAPTER 13

~ A Giant Step ~

After a week at home, Martin made a return visit to the hospital with his parents to see Dr Owens and Alan Green. Between them they had made some important decisions. There were to be no more operations. Martin had made up his mind: he'd had all the surgery he required and he wasn't going to have repeated stays in hospital trying to achieve a perfect face. He was thankful that there wasn't any rebuilding to be done and that the newly grafted skin had began to settle in. The very rough areas were now covered with new skin and the scars where the old met the new were less prominent. But Martin was still looking into mirrors at every opportunity, which worried Alan Green.

'Listen, Martin,' Alan said, 'looking in the mirror with confidence is great, but don't spend too much time doing it. Simply treat mirrors as you did before the operation.'

His mother turned to Alan with a knowing smile.

'Even before the accident he spent a lot of time looking in mirrors.'

Most importantly, Martin had decided that he was going to return to school on the first day of the new term. This was a giant step. Since the accident, Martin had only been in two buildings, the hospital and his home. The only people that he had interacted with had been hospital staff, his parents and his closest friends. Alan Green thought it was very worthy of Martin to want to go back to school but he was worried about him going back so soon. But Martin was adamant, he wanted to return to school at the start of term like everyone else.

That meeting was on Wednesday. The new term was to start on Monday and on Friday, when his father was at work and his mother was out visiting friends, the front doorbell rang. Martin was lying on his bed thinking of going back to school. He tiptoed carefully into the front room to see who it was through the front window. To Martin's astonishment it was Mr Lincoln, his form teacher. He was standing facing the door as stiffly as a soldier on parade. Martin wasn't sure what to do. He considered not opening the door, thinking that Mr Lincoln would come back another time when one of his parents was in, but then Mr Lincoln rang the bell again. Martin went out and opened the door.

'Hello, Martin, I hope you don't mind me calling. I would like a quick word if I may.'

Mr Lincoln looked Martin straight in the eyes. His minimalist smile was as good as Martin had ever seen it. He could also see that Mr Lincoln had come prepared.

'My mom and dad are not in but if you only need to speak to me that's OK.'

'I promise you, I'll be gone before you know it.'

As they entered the front room, Mr Lincoln began to talk about the weather. Martin noticed that he didn't ask how he was or how the holidays had gone. Eventually Mr Lincoln came to the point.

'Yesterday I had a talk with a Mr Alan Green, the clinical psychologist from Newham Parkside Hospital. He informed me that you wish to attend school on Monday. Is this correct?'

'Yes.'

'Are you sure that you want to do that? Do you realise I will have had no chance to prepare the class or the school? Most of the pupils and staff have seen the story in the local papers but let's face it . . . ' Mr Lincoln stopped suddenly, coughed and continued. 'I'm sorry. Let's be realistic. I am concerned about how your fellow pupils will react to you.'

'Well, Mr Lincoln, you shouldn't be afraid of using words like face – and look, I don't want any special treatment, I just want to continue my education. I don't see anything wrong with that.'

'There is nothing wrong with that at all but – ahem,' he coughed, 'but we cannot control the reaction of others.'

Martin was almost enjoying seeing Mr Lincoln struggling for words. 'What would you do if you had your way?' he enquired.

'Well, we would talk about your injuries in morning assembly before you arrived. We would let everyone know how impolite it is to stare and we would of course inform everyone that you are still the same person.'

'No way – my injuries, good manners and me are subjects that I happen to know a lot about. I can look after myself.'

'Very well.' Mr Lincoln spoke quietly. 'I'll see you on Monday then. Please don't hesitate to speak to me if you have any problems.'

As they headed towards the door, Martin said, 'I'm going to have to face the world soon. If I can't even face my school, then I have got problems.'

As soon as the door was shut, Martin ran up to his room, grabbed his little black book and ran back down to the phone to ring Natalie.

Natalie answered the phone. 'Hello.'

'Hi, Natalie, it's me, Martin. Guess what? I'm going to school on Monday.'

'Who said?' she asked, not hiding her surprise.

'I said. Tell Matthew and Mark. Come and call for me on your way. We can go together if that's cool.'

'Are you sure you want to go back so soon?'

'What do you mean, so soon? Everyone else is going back, so I'm going back.'

Natalie tried to express her concern carefully but it didn't work. 'You're not everyone else. You can't just rush into things now.'

Martin raised his voice. 'You're supposed to be supporting me, you should be helping me. What are friends for? I thought friends were supposed to stick together and help each other out.'

'OK, OK,' Natalie interrupted. 'I just think you should be taking it easy.'

'Will you knock for me on Monday morning or not?'

'Yes, I'll be there. I'll be speaking to Mark and Matthew later. See you on Monday.'

After the call Martin spent ten minutes standing by the phone. He considered ringing Natalie back and telling her not to bother coming on Monday. He wondered what it would be like walking to school. He couldn't understand why Natalie wasn't being the tower of strength that he expected her to be.

CHAPTER 14

~ New Beginnings ~

Monday morning was bright and sunny. Martin woke up to the smell of toast and the sound of the multitude of birds that ate, sang and danced in his back garden. Breakfast was as breakfast on school days used to be. His father ate too quickly and then rushed out of the house to catch his train whilst his mother tried throughout breakfast to convince his father to slow down. Martin, unable to understand why anyone would want to rush to a building to assemble radiators, ate his toast and wheatflakes without taking his eyes off the football magazine he was reading. When Natalie, Mark and Matthew turned up, it was like old times. His mother kissed him on the cheek and told him to take care of himself but she said nothing out of the ordinary. Martin was aware of this, and as they walked to school together, Martin was also aware of how ordinarily the other three were acting. But once they came out of the side street and on to the High Street things changed.

Martin immediately noticed people looking at him. Matthew struck up a conversation about the last day of school the term before, when Mark was licked by Jennifer Hamilton. Martin tried to involve himself but he was too busy watching people watching him and trying not to catch people's eyes at the same time. Martin could sense how many things had changed. He realised that he was no longer leading the gang, that the attention of the others was not gravitating towards him. He was not playing his usual tricks. Only halfway to school and it was the furthest Martin had walked for over a month. He could not tell who was staring or who was simply going about their business and just looking where they were going. He couldn't help thinking that everyone had read the papers, that everyone was staring. The people on the streets, the people in the shops, the people on the buses, the people in cars, all of them were looking at him.

Most of the pupils at Eastmorelands School had already heard about the accident from the press or their parents and friends, so when Martin arrived at the school, most made an effort not to make him feel uncomfortable. They arrived just as the bell rang, so they went straight into morning assembly. Religious assemblies had been stopped many years before at Eastmorelands. Assemblies now could be anything from a poetry reading to a story with a moral, or the headmistress waxing lyrical about how great the school could be if they all lived in unity and stopped chewing gum in class. Today she spoke of new beginnings. The way a day breaks, the way a seed germinates, the way you pick yourself up, dust yourself off and move forward. She spoke of these things with regard to the new term, and the new pupils, but Martin couldn't help feeling that much of what she said was said with him in mind.

In registration Mr Lincoln welcomed the class back and reminded them of the examinations they were soon to be having. 'I know it's been a difficult time for some of you but I do hope that some thought and study has been achieved over the holiday.'

Once again Martin thought that this was said with him in mind. *Who else has had a difficult time?* he asked himself. He for one had done absolutely no study. He had given the forthcoming examinations no thought. The class was a very different class now. Mark and Martin sat in their usual seats, well away from each other, but there were none of the usual wisecracks from Martin. His jokes were conspicuous by their absence, and the sound of laughter and Mr Lincoln's bellowing voice was replaced by an uncharacteristic order. Everyone, even Mr Lincoln, was on their best behaviour.

Martin's first full lesson was Science. He hated Science at the best of times and for his first lesson he would have preferred something a bit less interactive, an easier lesson where he would be able to relax and observe.

Once the class had settled, Mrs Malcolm the Science teacher announced, 'Today we shall be looking at why some materials dissolve in water and why others do not. First we shall be conducting some simple experiments, followed by a discussion about the results of these experiments. In order to carry out the experiments I need you to split up into pairs. Could you do that quickly and quietly now, please.'

The sound of whispers and shuffling chairs filled the room as people tried to pair up with their friends. Martin sat still. Neither Mark, Natalie or Matthew was in this lesson. Martin knew most of the pupils but he wasn't going to go looking for a partner. For a while he sat thinking that he would be the last to pair off when he was approached by Simon Hill. He was a thin ginger-haired boy who was known as 'the babble-mouth' because of his ability to speak volumes of rubbish.

'Me and you, Martin, yeah. Me and you, OK?'

'Yeah, that's cool,' Martin replied, although Simon wouldn't have been Martin's first choice for a partner.

Once the beakers, the jugs of water and the various other materials needed for the experiments were passed around, they began to follow the instructions of Mrs Malcolm. There were low level conversations going on between most of the pupils as tablets of salt, sugar and a variety of sodiums were added to water. Simon talked trivia relentlessly.

'On the way to school this morning I saw a red Ferrari, man, big wheels, sounded like a rocket, guy. Lee Hendrie, he plays for Aston Villa, he got a red Ferrari too. I saw a black one once but they're not as good as red ones, I don't think. If I was going to get a black car, I'd get a Porsche 911, they're good in black, but Ferraris should be red. What do you reckon?'

'Yeah, you're right. Ferraris are best red.' Martin was not very enthusiastic. He did use to love red Ferraris but his love of cars had brought him enough trouble. But Simon continued.

'Yeah, man, when I get the chance I'm going to get a red Ferrari but if I get married and my bird wants a Porsche, I'll get a black one to keep her happy like, you know – girls like Porsches. I saw a wicked video last night, it was called *Fearless Mind*. It was about a man who didn't like nobody, man. He killed thirty people in thirty minutes, but he didn't kill just one person a minute. Sometimes he killed no one for a few minutes, then he killed lots of people in one minute. It was good, blood everywhere. There was one bit when the star, his name was Fearless, well, he put his gun up this other man's nostril and blew his brains out.'

Martin had now heard enough. He wasn't going to

create a disturbance but he felt he had to put a stop to Simon's out of control babbling.

'Listen, I don't wanna know 'bout any film. Give it a rest. Let's just do our work.'

'Yeah, you're right,' Simon replied. 'Let's work. But I'm telling you, I don't mind sitting by you and working with you, not like some people. I don't care if you look a bit poxy.'

Martin was filled with rage; his eyes watered with anger. He felt his temperature rise, as he stepped back and looked Simon up and down in disgust.

'Who you calling poxy?'

Simon backed off. 'I know you're not poxy. I just said I don't care if you look a bit poxy.'

Martin couldn't control himself any longer. He threw a punch that connected with Simon's chin and sent him over the table they were using. The paraphernalia that was on the table flew in all directions, causing some pupils to dive for cover. Martin wasted no time. He dived on Simon and a rolling scrap ensued.

Mrs Malcolm screamed at the top of her voice. 'Stop it at once, you two,' but they continued. Eventually Mrs Malcolm and some of the pupils managed to get in between the tables and separate the pair.

Martin's hand was in great pain from the first blow he threw, as was Simon's chin. There were no major injuries but both of them were soaked with water from the experiments and needed to be held apart from each other.

'I'll kill you,' Martin fumed.

'I'll kill you first – no, I don't even need to kill you. You'll kill yourself because you're a drug head guy and everyone knows you take drugs – you're a loser.'

The veins on Martin's neck stood out. He surged forward towards Simon kicking tables and chairs as he went, in an amazing burst of aggression. 'I'll kill you. I ain't no drug head, you don't know anything about me. I'll tear you apart.'

Martin had found extra strength but Mrs Malcolm and her helpers managed to hold Martin back. Even he realised that the rage he had unleashed was awesome.

Mrs Malcolm shouted at the top of her voice, 'Right, Simon Hill, go and stand outside the classroom door until I'm ready for you.'

Martin was sat down and allowed to cool.

By the time the classroom floor had been cleared and tables and chairs put back into place, the lesson was nearly over. Simon and Martin were ordered to see the headmistress at lunch time and they went their ways. For Martin's next lesson, English, he was reunited with Mark and Matthew.

As they entered the classroom, Mark asked Martin, 'What happened in Science, man?'

'Simon Hill, man. That weird kid – upset me big time.'

'What did he do?' Matthew asked.

'I'll tell you later,' Martin said as they went to their seats.

At lunch time Simon and Martin waited outside the headmistress's office. They were both tense – not a single word was said by either of the boys. They totally ignored each other. Then Mrs Powell the headmistress called them into her office.

'The first hour of the first morning of the new term and we already have a fight in school – we certainly cannot continue in this manner,' she told the boys as they both gazed towards their shoes. 'So what happened?'

Simon told his side of the story in his roundabout way and then Martin told his. Both were accurate accounts of the event from their own points of view. Mrs Powell walked over to the boys and stood at arm's length in front of them. 'Now, Simon, you and everyone else have to understand that Martin has no disease and no one in school or out of school has ever found Martin carrying drugs. If that rumour is going around the school it must stop.'

She looked towards Martin. 'And you, Martin, you have to control your temper. People may say all kinds of things. People will react to you in different ways but you cannot go hitting everybody who upsets you. Mr Green from the hospital and Mr Lincoln your form teacher have both told you and now I'm telling you. If you need help, come to one of us.'

'But miss . . . ' Martin protested. 'It's not me that needs help, it's him and his big mouth. He needs help.'

'Martin,' Mrs Powell interrupted, 'under the circumstances I'm going to let you both off. We'll just call it a misunderstanding, shall we?'

'Yes, miss,' Simon replied.

'Yes, miss,' said Martin.

'But don't let it happen again. I don't want to see either of you in my office for the rest of the term. Now shake hands and go to lunch.'

Martin and Simon shook hands slowly and cautiously, without looking directly at each other or saying a word.

In the dining hall Martin still felt staring eyes upon him. He sat in the safe company of Mark, Matthew and Natalie and outside in the playground he stayed with them. Most of the pupils were polite and were trying to show Martin that they were still his friends. Some were just too polite. Either way Martin was very aware that he was being treated differently. He survived the rest of the day by getting on with his work and trying to ignore the sights and sounds around him. It was a long day.

As he was leaving school that afternoon with Mark, Matthew and Natalie, Natalie asked him what had happened in the Science lesson. Martin told them the story. All three were surprised. 'I've never seen you have a scrap,' Natalie said.

'Well, you've never seen me stuck with Simon Hill,' Martin replied.

As they walked down the street, Martin was approached by a girl. He had seen her a couple of times before in school but he had never spoken to her.

'Hello, Martin,' she said. 'I just wanted to give you this.'

She handed him an envelope and walked away. Martin could see it was a card and so could Natalie. 'Aren't you going to open it then?' Natalie said suspiciously.

'Later.' Martin put it in the inside pocket of his jacket and his friends walked him to his house before going their separate ways.

When Martin arrived home he opened the envelope in his bedroom. Without even opening the card to see the name of the girl, he threw the card in the bin in a moment of hurt and anguish and shouted, 'I'm not ill – I'm not bloody ill.' The front of the card said *Get Well Soon*.

CHAPTER 15

~ The Voice of Reason ~

One day in school had taught Martin a lot. That evening he listened to no music, and he spent no time looking at pictures of footballers. Instead he spent the whole evening in his room in quiet contemplation. He was now beginning to look at *himself* in before and after terms. Ever since he had first woken up in hospital after the accident, he had begun to listen to a voice of reason in his head. It was an honest voice, a voice that had nothing to gain by taking sides. Back then it had started as a whisper but now the voice was loud.

Knowing that he had hundreds of days left to attend school, he began his meditation by asking himself one question. *How can I improve on today?* He considered the Simon Hill affair and promised himself not to lose his temper if he ever got into a similar situation. He thought about what Mrs Powell had said in morning assembly and what Mr Lincoln had said in registration, then he promised himself that he wouldn't read too much into people's words. He thought, *maybe they weren't talking about me.* And *maybe*, he thought, *all those people in the streets and their cars, and on the buses, maybe they weren't all looking at me.* He walked over to the full-length mirror on his wardrobe and looked at himself. *So what if they were looking at me?* he asked himself. *Two months ago, if I'd seen me looking like I look now, I would have had a good look. Be honest, Mr Martin Turner, you would have probably made some remark, or even cracked a joke with your friends.*

The next day Martin went back to school with a sense of purpose. At lunch time he found the girl who had given him the get well card and told her as she was eating, 'I'm sure you didn't want to offend me, so thanks for the card but you should know that I am well.'

'I'm sorry,' she said. 'I read about you in the papers, I really felt for you.'

'OK. I just want you to know that I'm not sick.'

'Point taken. I'm sorry. Are we friends?' she enquired.

'Yeah, friends are cool.'

He chose not to speak to Simon Hill but he also decided not to make him an enemy. Rumours were continuing to spread about the role of drugs in the accident but Martin displayed a positive attitude and carried on regardless.

The days felt much longer than they used to. Martin counted the hours and the lessons as they passed. He was less self-conscious about his face but he made sure it wasn't going to stop him doing what he wanted to do, including his favourite pastime at school – gymnastics. He hardly felt any pain now. Most of the time he was only reminded of his new face when he touched it or when others stared.

On Wednesday the whole school was talking about him for something completely different. That morning he took Year 10 by storm with a stunning gymnastics display, first on the trampoline and then on the floor mat, his speciality. Some of the old fun-loving Martin appeared when, at the end of a fantastic floor mat routine, he entertained the crowd with a mixture of comical dance and gymnastics. Martin left school that day high-spirited. When he told his parents about his display that evening, they began to feel that Martin was quickly and happily adjusting to life in school.

Thursday morning went well for Martin. He was beginning to enjoy lessons like never before. Teachers and many of his fellow pupils could see that he was now keen to learn. He was showing a genuine interest in subjects and although he was not the prankster he used to be he was beginning to relax.

At lunch time Martin made his way to the dining room and collected his meal. After picking up his drink, he looked for his friends but Natalie was sitting with a group of her girlfriends. She waved to him but he could see that there was no room there. Certainly there was no room for a boy. On the other side of the hall he could see Mark and Matthew. He began to walk in their direction but as he reached them he could see there were no free seats there either.

'Where have you been?' Matthew asked.

'I had to go and check something out in the library,' Martin replied.

Matthew looked around and, seeing spare seats elsewhere, said, 'Well, we're almost finished. Find a seat somewhere and we'll see you afterwards.'

Martin looked around. He saw a group of boys and girls from his class sitting close, so he went over and sat down. 'All right,' Martin said to them as he sat down.

There was a collective 'All right' from everyone on the table and they all continued to eat. All seemed to be going well until Margaret Knight, the girl sitting opposite him, threw down her knife and fork and exclaimed, 'Why did you sit here?'

Martin's response was quick. 'Because it's a seat and I wanna eat me dinner. This is the dinning hall, isn't it? What's your problem?'

'You're my problem,' she replied. 'You're putting me off my food.'

Martin could feel his temperature rising but the voice in his head reminded him of his promise to stay cool. Instead of all out war, Martin began a war of words with her.

'You put lots of people off their food with your smelly breath but we've all got to eat to live.'

'Why don't you sit with your friends? They're used to you.'

'Why don't you sit on your own?' Martin replied with a grin.

'I was here before you. Look, there's lots of empty seats. Why did you come to spoil my dinner?'

'I can sit anywhere I want. Ain't no rules about where people sit as long as it's on a chair with a table in front of it. So if you've got a problem, go and get advice – I'm not moving.'

Margaret picked up her tray and stood up. 'I was going anyway. I don't have to sit here and let you talk to me like that.' She walked off, emptied her tray and left the hall.

Martin didn't eat much. He remembered promising himself not to lose his temper in times like these, but he was really upset by what had just happened. Only the scraping of plates and chewing of gum could be heard. Nobody knew what to say.

After the meal, outside in the playground, Martin was approached by Najma Khan. 'Can I have a word with you, Martin?' she asked.

'Yeah, but I'm warning you, if you want to go raving tomorrow night – I'm busy – I'm washing me hair.'

Najma smiled. 'Oh what a shame. Seriously now – I just wanted to say that Margaret didn't really mean what she said earlier. She asked me to say sorry for her.'

Martin was not convinced. 'If she's that sorry, why didn't she say sorry herself?'

'She's not very good at talking, so she sent me.'

'She had lots of mouth in the dinner hall,' Martin said. 'She's what I call a facialist. She's dealing in facial discrimination.'

'Well, she told me that she has nothing against you personally and that she just gets put off her food easily.'

'And what do you think about that, Najma?'

'I think she's being stupid,' Najma replied, 'but that's the way she is. I'm always telling her how silly she can be.'

'Well, you tell her some more,' Martin said as he walked away. 'Tell her I said she's a facialist and if she's got anything else she wants to tell me – tell her to tell me herself. By the way, I'm sorry about tomorrow night – maybe some other time.'

For the rest of the day, every time Margaret Knight saw Martin, she hid herself or turned around and went another way.

The next day was trouble-free, a day of Maths, History, Geography and Biology. It was Friday, and Martin had had a week of ups and downs. He was very much looking forward to the weekend. At the end of the day, the Gang of Three and Natalie met at the school gate and began to make their way to Martin's house. The other three felt protective towards Martin and although it was never planned, each one felt that the least they could do in the early days of the term was to make sure he got home all right. Martin was aware of this trend and he easily guessed why they escorted him every afternoon. He also realised that walking home alone on those first few days would have been very different without them.

As they walked down the High Street, Natalie made an announcement. 'Right, you three,' she said, stopping suddenly and taking the gang by surprise. 'I've got something to tell you.'

'I know what it is,' Martin said jokingly. 'You're gonna buy us all a present for being your friend.'

'No,' Natalie replied laughing.

Mark thought that he should have a go. 'I know . . . you're . . . you're . . . you're gonna be rich.'

'No, almost.'

'Come on,' Martin insisted. 'Tell us.'

'Well,' Natalie said. 'You remember that hair shampoo commercial that I done?'

The boys all nodded frantically.

'The company that I did the commercial for want me to do another one. I am playing the same person – just a bit older. Do you know what that means?'

Matthew tried to be funny. 'Yes, it means you're playing the same person – just a bit older.'

Natalie was almost jumping with excitement. 'Yes, but what's more important is that if they want me to play the same person that's a bit older, then they'll probably want me to do it again and again and again. I'll become known as the Nulocks girl.'

'So you *will* be rich,' Mark interrupted.

'Maybe, I don't know. The money goes into a trust and I get it when I am eighteen or something like that.'

Matthew and Mark congratulated her. Martin wasn't so sure. 'Do you really want to be known as the Nulocks girl?'

'That will only be for a time,' Natalie replied. 'The agent said that the main thing is that it's a high profile commercial, shown all over the world, and it'll get me even better work in the future.'

'I suppose that's not bad,' Martin replied half-heartedly. 'The problem is, I've heard of a thing called typecasting. It's where you get known for only one type of thing and no one wants you to work for them unless you're doing that one thing.'

'Now look who's not being supportive!' Natalie snapped. 'What did you say friends were for again? You know this is a good chance for me and all you can do is criticise. Stop thinking about yourself for once, Martin. Why don't you try wishing me good luck?'

'I do wish you good luck but I'm just trying to warn you about the business.'

'What do you know about the business? You don't know anything,' she said angrily. She took a breath and continued, 'I'm young, so as long as I don't do too much of one thing I'll have time to change. That's what my agent said and she should know.'

'Yeah, she should know,' Matthew interjected in an effort to calm things down.

'That's right,' Natalie agreed.

'Forget it. Just make sure that you remember us when you're rich and famous,' Mark added as they continued their journey home.

After their evening meal, Martin's parents asked him how his week had been. He told them about the fight he had had with Simon Hill, only to discover that they already knew about it. At this point Martin realised that during the week, many eyes had been watching him.

'I've been speaking to the headmistress,' his father said. 'She told me that if you need some more time off, you should take it.'

'I'm OK,' Martin replied. 'I'm not ill, my brain's working OK and I can hold a pen in my hand and write. So I don't see no reason why I should not go to school.'

As Martin's father was leaving the dinner table he

placed his hand on Martin's head and asked, 'What are you doing over the weekend, son?

Martin stood up and replied, 'Homework,' and then he went up to his room.

CHAPTER 16

~ The Problem With Unity ~

Martin learnt quickly to take every day as it came and never to expect one day to be the same as the last. His fellow pupils could be unpredictable: some would want to show how good they were by being seen with him, others would use him as the butt of their jokes or avoid contact with him. Some kids could be both caring and uncaring according to their mood, or whose company they were in. He was beginning to choose his friends according to the respect they had for him. He hated being pitied and he hated being given special treatment. He learnt how to look into the eyes of others and measure their sincerity.

October became very rainy. It put a stop to much of the school's outdoor activities but the rain was much needed after the dry, hot summer. There was a lot of talk in school about Natalie's new commercial. She was becoming a minor celebrity. When Martin saw the commercial, he realised why everyone was talking about it so much. It started with Natalie washing her hair, with an extra large bottle of Nulocks Shampoo in the foreground. Then a shot of her drying her hair, followed by quick flashes of her meeting a friend in a bus station. As they jumped on the bus, the camera focused on her bouncy, flowing hair. Then there was a shot of them in a club dancing with two boys. The other girl's hair began to look tired but Natalie's hair, washed with new improved Nulocks, still looked 'fresh and bouncy', as the voice-over said.

Martin thought the commercial was good and that it was sure to help Natalie's future career in acting or modelling. But seeing her as the centre of attention in the commercial and knowing how popular she had now become in school highlighted the change in their relationship. They still talked, they still spent time together, but that time was always in the company of others. They had not kissed since the night of the accident. It wasn't every afternoon now that Natalie walked Martin home with Mark and Matthew, and she never walked him home alone. In fact, all four of them would sometimes go their separate ways at the school gate.

Martin had the confidence now to walk home on his own. Walking home via the same route at the same time meant that he would usually be seen by the same people. It didn't take long for most people to get used to seeing him. It was the same in the mornings on the way to school. These were becoming Martin's safe zones.

Martin also began to wonder about his relationship with Matthew and Mark. He didn't doubt that they were still friends. He knew that he was no longer the 'main man' but he was conscious of other changes. There was a time when Mark wanted to be with Martin at every opportunity – this wasn't so now. He began to hang out with a couple of other boys. It was as if he was making a new gang, with himself as the leader. Matthew was different, he still spent some time with Martin but he now preferred to be alone. Martin thought maybe Matthew was using the cir-cumstances to take a step back and become himself. He just hoped that Matthew would be there if he needed him.

On a wet Friday afternoon after school, Natalie and the Gang of Three were standing at the school gate talking to friends. Martin thought it was a good time to suggest something that he had been thinking about for a while. 'Hey, let's go out somewhere together this weekend.'

There was a moment's silence, as if they were all a little surprised by Martin's suggestion. He had shown no real interest in going out since returning to school and none of them had given the idea any thought.

Natalie was the first to respond. 'I got drama school tomorrow and dance class on Sunday. I won't have any time this weekend.'

Mark's response was unconvincing. 'I'm not sure. Where we going to go? What we going to do? I just wanna stay in and watch some movies.'

Matthew's response was the only positive one and even that was conditional. 'I'll go out but I'm not going to one of those rave or rap places.'

'That's cool, man, we'll just go out, walk around East Ham or something. Check me at my house around seven.'

At seven o'clock the next evening, Matthew arrived at Martin's house. As he went to press the bell, the door opened. It was Martin's father.

'Hello, Mr Turner.'

'Ssh, be quiet,' Martin's father whispered. Matthew couldn't work out what was happening as Mr Turner pushed him outside and closed the door gently behind them both. 'I wanna word with you – now, you know the phone number here, don't you?'

'Yes, Mr Turner,' Matthew replied.

'Well, you look after Martin, it's his first night out. If there's any trouble, give me a ring straight away – I'm sure he can look after himself, but if there's a problem ring me – all right?' he said, trying hard to keep his voice down.

When they entered the house, Martin's father rang the bell to make Martin think Matthew had just arrived, then he shouted upstairs, 'Martin, are you ready? Matthew's here.'

Martin ran down the stairs, heavy-footed and ready to go. Tonight he was wearing his black shell suit and black baseball cap with his white trainers. Without giving Matthew a chance to settle down, he shouted, 'We're off, Mom, see you later. Bye, Dad.'

Matthew bid Mr and Mrs Turner goodbye and they headed down the street. There was a spring in Martin's step. Before Matthew had arrived, just thinking about going out into the night made him nervous. Now he wasn't worrying, he was just happy to be out and about. He would have liked to have been with the whole gang, including Natalie, but he still appreciated Matthew's company.

At eight o'clock in the evening High Street North was very different. All the school children were missing, the sweet shops were shut and the familiar faces had all gone. The restaurants, bars and amusement arcades had now come to life. For a while Martin became self-conscious again but he quickly realised that everyone was too busy doing their own thing to notice him.

'Where shall we go?' he asked Matthew. 'You said no

raves and no rap, so that doesn't leave much, does it?'

'I have an idea,' said Matthew. 'Let's go the Unity.'

Martin's voice raised and changed to a higher key. 'Are you kidding, guy, the Unity, table tennis and bingo, come on, man – things aren't that bad.'

'Well, what do you suggest?' Matthew replied.

'I don't know but there's got to be somewhere better than that.'

'Name it.'

'I don't know what scenes are happening.'

'All the happening scenes are full of drugs and losers. When I go out nowadays all I wanna do is get home safely – and getting home safely usually depends on where you go – so I've got no problem with the Unity.'

'I suppose you're right and I suppose I should know better. OK, to the Unity we go.'

On the way to the Unity, Martin began to confide in Matthew. 'I'll tell you something, mate, just because this has happened to me I won't let it hold me back. I'm not going to sit at home feeling sorry for myself, I'm going to go out and get some.'

'Yeah,' Matthew replied. 'But what you gonna get some of? Do you wanna get some of those fast cars?'

Martin stopped walking. Matthew stopped a step ahead of him. 'What you trying to say, Matthew, man? Don't you think I've learnt anything lately? Or are you just trying to upset me or something?'

'Why would I want to upset you? I just think cars are trouble. And most of that music you listen to is all about guns and drugs and girls.'

Martin was quick to defend. 'Cars are OK, it's people who are crazy, and not all rap music is bad. I like it for the beat, man, the grooves. You know I never used to like rap music but it's cool to dance to. I don't listen to all that stuff about guns and drugs. The stuff about girls is cool. I got no problem with that. It's just fun, man, don't tell me girls are out of fashion!'

They both continued to walk as Matthew spoke. 'No, but you know what I mean, it's all about lust and not about love.'

Martin's mood changed and he laughed as he said, 'What are you saying, man? What have you been reading? We ain't supposed to fall in love until we're twenty-one or something like that. Love is something you fall into when you gotta job.'

Matthew stopped laughing. 'Do you seriously mean that?'

'No,' Martin began to cool down. 'I don't really mean it, but you sound so serious about it. Love's OK but lust is fun.'

'Isn't lust sin? Anyway, what are you dealing with? Do you love Natalie or do you lust her?' Matthew enquired.

Martin stopped laughing. 'Good question. Well, you see, it's a bit of both, it's half love and half lust and if we go out together for a long time, the half lust will grow into love, that's when we'll do the marriage and baby thing.'

For a few yards there was silence. What Martin had said had got Matthew thinking and Martin was also thinking about what he had just said. Martin began to get even more personal.

'Tell me the truth now, Matthew. Do you think Natalie still likes me?'

'Of course she does,' Matthew replied.

'Do girls lust?' Martin asked.

'I've heard that they do at certain times of the year – I think there is a season when they get all hot and passionate or something.'

'Well, do you think she loves me or anything like that?'

'I'm not too sure what you mean by anything like that, and from what you've just said we're all too young to know what love is.'

But Martin came again with more questions. 'Do you think she's gone off me since the accident? Has she said anything to you about me?'

Matthew could see that deep down Martin was desperate for the truth. 'Listen, Martin,' Matthew replied, 'honest to God – I don't know if she's gone off you or not – I don't think so – but I don't know. And she hasn't said anything to me. When she talks to me about you it's always about making sure you're OK, making sure you get home OK and making sure you stay out of trouble.'

'So,' Martin replied as if slightly surprised, 'she cares about me.'

They reached the Unity club to find about fifteen kids there. Two games of table tennis were being played. A small group of boys were playing computerised football. A group of four girls were looking through a fashion magazine and one boy was playing chess with Tony the priest. These were the good kids of the neighbourhood. All were dressed sensibly and on their best behaviour.

Tony waved and shouted, 'Hello, Martin, nice to see you. Hi, Matthew.'

Matthew waved and Martin nodded his head in response. They watched the boys playing computerised football. Some of the younger kids stared at Martin out of curiosity but they were quietly told off by their older friends. Martin could hear the whispered telling offs as he explored the various corners of the club.

He hated it. After thirty minutes he told Matthew how much he hated it. 'Look, man, we got to go. I hate it here. Lying in a hospital bed is more exciting. Let's go.'

'Where?' Matthew asked.

'Anywhere. I'd rather just walk the streets than stay here.'

'OK,' Matthew said. 'Let's go.'

As they reached the door, Tony jumped up from his seat and ran over to them. Martin had always found him funny with his very posh accent and his out of date sense of fashion. Tonight he was dressed in jeans, a tweed jacket and a white shirt with his church collar on top of it.

'Martin, my dear friend,' he said. 'It's good to see you. Aren't you staying?'

'No, I can't,' Martin replied. 'I promised my parents I'd be home early tonight.'

'I understand. I've been seeing quite a lot of Matthew lately, haven't I, Matthew?'

'Yes,' Matthew said reluctantly.

Martin shifted his eyes towards Matthew in surprise.

'Matthew knows that he's welcome to come here any time – so are you. Our doors are open to anyone regardless of age, race – or disability.'

Martin's heart raced. He breathed deeply in order to control his temper. He felt sweat breaking out in his palms and a warm glow around him as if his blood was warming. Once again he felt like lashing out; he didn't care if he was a priest, he wanted to punch him. But the voice in his head said, *No. Just talk to him.*

'Tony, you listen to me, man. You may think you're perfect, you may think you know everything and that you're going to Heaven but let me tell ya something, I ain't disabled.'

149

Tony tried to interrupt. 'I didn't say you were disabled. I just said all are welcome regardless of race or . . .'

Martin came back, 'Disability. You've never mentioned age or race to me before. Why you quoting your equal opportunity stuff to me now; I've been coming to this place a long time before you.'

'Calm down now, Martin,' Tony held his hands out and waved them soothingly. 'Calm down.'

'I am calm. Let me explain something to you. Anything I could do before I can do now. There are some things I can do better now, like spotting the patroniser. I was in here two months ago, I'm only two months older now, and I am the same race and I have the same abilities. Goodnight, Mister – Reverend – Tony.'

Martin turned and walked away at speed. Matthew was stunned by Martin's performance. For a moment he watched Martin walking down the road, then he looked at Tony, who was also in a state of shock, watching Martin.

'I've got to go,' Matthew said and he ran to join Martin. When Matthew had caught up with him he was out of breath. 'Hey, Martin, that was amazing, man. I like the way you just come out with the truth, man.'

Martin replied on the move with his tongue firmly in check. 'This is part of my role in life – you see, some people may think I've got some disease that they can catch, or that the way I look makes me disabled, so I have to tell people to look beneath my face and see me, the real me. This is deep.'

They walked back to Martin's house at a leisurely pace. Martin asked Matthew why he had been spending so much time at the Unity and how he put up with their lack of activities. Matthew agreed that the club wasn't the liveliest of places but he insisted that it was safe and there was never any trouble there.

Martin went to bed contented that night. The idea that he might be seen as disabled angered him greatly, but recalling Tony's response, or lack of response to his outburst, amused him. He also realised that living with his new looks could well mean that he had to become an educator. *It isn't just about me and how I cope with it, it's me learning to deal with other people's prejudices*, he thought.

CHAPTER 17

~ The Call of Duty ~

Martin spent Sunday lazing around the house listening to music and trying to convince his father that buying him a pair of trainers that cost £100 was a good investment. His father spent Sunday telling Martin to leave him alone and Mrs Turner tried hard to keep the peace. It was very much like old times.

Martin woke up early on Monday morning. He made his own breakfast of egg on toast before heading off to school.

As he approached the school he saw Matthew waiting. On seeing Martin, Matthew began to walk towards him. Martin could sense that something wasn't right.

'Hi, man. What's up?' Martin asked.

'Have you seen the local paper?'

'You know I don't read the papers,' Martin replied.

Matthew pulled a newspaper from out of a bag he had over his shoulder. '*Newham Echo*, guy, front page. Look.'

Matthew held the front page up for Martin to see and Martin read it out loud. '**Drug Crazed Car Thief Goes to Jail**.' Martin grabbed the paper from Matthew and began to read the report.

'A nineteen-year-old man appeared before Snaresbrook Court on Monday on eight counts of taking motor vehicles without the owners' permission and four charges of supplying heroin. Graham Fisher, who was known to his associates as The Apache, was described by Judge Murray Cole as a mindless, selfish beast who had no regard for the rule of law and therefore had to be removed from the free world for the protection of upright citizens.

The court heard how in August, Fisher and Peter Mosley (17), stole a Ford Escort from Katherine Road in East Ham and picked up two younger boys on the Boleyn Estate. They were later spotted by a police patrol car travelling at 100 mph. The police gave chase at high speed, resulting in a crash at the junction of Green Street and Barking Road. Peter Mosley was announced dead at the scene of the crash. Mark Thorpe (15) and Graham Fisher both received minor injuries but Martin Turner (15) was so badly burnt that he was hospitalised and had to undergo plastic surgery. The court heard that Martin Turner and his school friend Mark Thorpe were unaware that the car was stolen and believed they were receiving a lift home. But Graham Fisher, who had earlier used a large amount of heroin, instead went on a high speed drive through Newham and Essex. After the arrest of Fisher, it was discovered that both he and Mosley were members of a gang known as The Raiders Posse. Various other members of the gang have since been arrested and charged with drug and firearms offences. Sentencing Fisher to three years' imprisonment for car theft, Judge Murray Cole said that young people must learn that they cannot simply take what is not theirs without suffering the consequences of the law. Fisher broke down in court and cried when the judge sentenced him to a further three years' imprisonment for the possession of, and supplying, drugs. The sentences are to run consecutively.'

Martin stopped reading and looked towards Matthew. 'What's consecutive mean?'

'It means that when one sentence finishes, the other starts. Really he got six years.

Did you read all of it?'

'No.'

'Read on.'

Martin continued to read. 'The judge ordered that Fisher stay in prison for the full sentence with no chance of remission or parole. He went on to say that the sentence was a light one. Given that someone was killed and another young boy was scarred for life, he said that Fisher should count himself lucky he wasn't facing a manslaughter charge.'

'Wow, heavy stuff, man.' Martin handed the paper back to Matthew. His eyes looked glazed as he stared into nothingness. 'Six years to the day, supplying heroin.'

'It could have been manslaughter, guy,' Matthew responded. 'It could have been fifteen or twenty years or something – anyway, man, everyone's talking about it.'

In assembly that morning, Mrs Powell gave another lecture. This time it was about the youth of today being the leaders of tomorrow. 'If the young people of our nation do not have self-control and consideration for others, we face a future of anarchy,' she said. 'We must not live in the past but we must learn from our experiences, recognise our responsibilities and learn to say no when temptation comes our way.'

Mr Lincoln stood at the side of the hall nodding like a toy dog. Martin knew that the headmistress had also been reading the local papers and he had expected her to use the case as the basis of her talk but he hated the fact that everyone's eyes turned towards him. Mark went unnoticed because he had no visible scars, but Martin had no choice in the matter. He represented the living and the dead because he was the most visible.

It was a bad start to a day that seemed to drag on for ages. At lunch time, Martin ate alone, as Mark was busy impressing his new friends, Natalie ate with her girlfriends and Matthew was nowhere to be seen. When it was time to go home it was much the same. Martin felt betrayed. This was the time when he needed moral support and there was no one there. He convinced himself that it wasn't because they were no longer his friends, but because they were all just too busy. As he began to make his way home, he heard somebody calling him.

'Turner, Turner!'

Martin turned back to see Mr Hewitt the PE teacher running towards him. Mr Hewitt couldn't be anything else but a PE teacher. He was over six foot, and dressed in a tracksuit.

'I've been looking for you, Turner. I want to ask you something,' he said looking down on Martin.

'Me, sir?'

'Yes, you, sir. I have been asked to put a gymnastics team together for a local competition at the Newham Leisure Centre next month, so I need to ask you two favours.'

'Me, sir?'

'Yes, you, sir.'

'What, sir?' Martin was genuinely puzzled.

'I want you to be in the team.'

'Oh yes, sir,' Martin said excitedly. 'I'll do some moves – but what else do you want, sir?'

'I want you to be the captain of the team.'

Martin's excitement changed to disbelief. 'What, me, sir? Why me, sir?'

Mr Hewitt poked Martin's shoulder with a sharp finger. 'Because you, Mr Martin Turner, are the best gymnast we have in the school . . . because you, Mr Martin Turner, have leadership qualities and because you, Mr Martin Turner, have earnt it.'

'Me?' Martin was seriously happy. He produced a big smile. 'Me, sir, honest, sir?'

'Yes, yes, yes, you, sir. Honest, sir.'

'It's a deal.' Martin put his hand out for the shake and Mr Hewitt did the same. They shook hands frantically and said their goodbyes. Martin then ran home at full speed. Happiness radiated from him.

When he arrived home, his mother was preparing a meal. He ran up to her and kissed her on both cheeks. 'Guess what, Mom, I'm the chosen one. I'm the main man. I'm the captain.'

'Calm down, Martin.' His mother couldn't understand a word. 'What have you won?'

'I haven't won anything really, not yet anyway, but I'm the captain. I'm the captain of the gymnastics team.'

'Oh, well done,' his mother replied. 'Does it mean you get paid then?'

'No, Mom, it means that I'm the leader. I have to set an example, you know. It means that I'm . . . it means I'm the main man.'

His mother put her arm around his shoulder and hugged him. 'I know what it means, silly. I was just pulling your gymnastic leg. Well done, lad.'

When his father arrived home, Martin ran down from his room to tell him. As always, his father showed little emotion. 'That's very good, son,' he said, patting him on his head. 'Gymnastics, is that like ballet?'

CHAPTER 18

~ Dancemania Revisited ~

The new captain of the gymnastics team took his job very seriously. He helped in the selection of the team, he helped organise training sessions and he helped to keep the morale of the team high when the going got tough. Everyone around Martin was aware of how enthusiastic he was about the gymnastics team and the competition.

Word spread quickly about Martin being captain. There were many people in the squad older than him but no one could dispute his ability. The team trained twice weekly and when possible Mr Hewitt would organise out of hours training; on top of this, Martin was practising his moves whenever he could. He had to work hard to get back to his normal level of fitness. If he couldn't fully practise the moves, he would stretch as much as he could and exercise to keep in shape. He worked out a routine that he would do in the mornings before breakfast. Twenty sit-ups, twenty press-ups. Left foot on dressing table for a five minute stretch, right foot on dressing table for a five minute stretch. Down on floor for five minutes in full splits position. Then breakfast. After breakfast, kick left leg in the air ten times, then repeat with the right leg. Rotate head five times in a circular motion to the left, then five to the right. Forward five times, then back five. Then, to strengthen his calf muscles, he would stand flat on his feet and push forward on to his tip-toes forty times, until it burnt. This was followed by a five minute lie on his bed to do some deep breathing and then he would run like crazy to the toilet. Before he went to sleep at night he did a similar routine.

When Martin started training with the team, everybody could see the scars on his legs. He had to spend a lot of time demonstrating techniques but he always felt at ease. The team became his new gang, and their success was his new ambition. Some believed that after Natalie's acting success, Martin's gymnastic ambitions were only an attempt to impress her. But Martin knew differently.

Eastmorelands concentrated on football and cricket for the boys, so those who liked gymnastics had to wait for opportunities such as these competitions. Martin knew the standard competition routine well, and he knew that to really stand out from the other seven schools in the competition he would have to think up something very imaginative for the free-form display. For the first two weeks of preparation Mr

Hewitt and Martin made sure the team focused on the usual competition disciplines. After a training session at which Martin and Mr Hewitt could see that the trampoline, the horse, the floor and the other disciplines were going well, Martin made a suggestion to Mr Hewitt.

'Sir, you know our free-form routine? I got this idea. I wanna do a hip-hop dance thing, a kinda funky gymnastics with some bad beats going down.'

Mr Hewitt looked very confused but he tried hard not to show it. It took him a few seconds before his mind grasped the concept. 'Right, I see. Hip-hop and funky gymnastics with some bad beats.'

'That's right, sir. That's bad meaning good type bad, sir.'

'I'm not sure, Martin. It sounds good, my kids would love it but I've never seen anything like that before in a competition.'

'But sir, in Art, in Drama, even in English, teachers say that originality brings progress. Why not in gymnastics?'

'Because the judges will be looking for good executions of techniques in the various disciplines.'

'But sir, this is free-form.'

Mr Hewitt was won over by Martin's argument and his enthusiasm. 'OK,' he said. 'At the end of each training session, I'll leave you to work out your funky, hip-hop dance thing. Just don't do anything dangerous.'

'That's wicked, sir. Thanks,' Martin replied. Then he went off to introduce his ideas to the other members of the team.

Saturday morning, as he lay in a soapy bathtub considering the meaning of life, love and lust, Martin asked himself, *Where do you really want to go tonight?* When he had ruled out the Unity club, the Psycho club and many other places he never really enjoyed, there was only one place left. DANCEMANIA. Then he asked himself, *Who shall I go with?* He concluded that Mark was history, Matthew was a nonstarter but Natalie, she just might. It had been her idea to go there before. Maybe she would be interested in a return visit together as boyfriend and girlfriend. Martin jumped out of the bath, wrapped a towel around himself and, still dripping wet, grabbed his little black book and went to phone Natalie. He stood in the hallway wetting the carpet and phone as his parents watched breakfast TV in the living room.

He dialled. The phone rang. The phone was answered: it was Natalie's father. Martin deepened his voice. 'Err, hello. Could I speak to Natalie Hepburn please?'

'May I ask who's speaking?'

'Certainly, it's Mr Turner from CBTV.'

'Oh, hold the line, please, she will be with you in a moment,' Mr Hepburn replied.

'Hello, this is Natalie Hepburn. Who's speaking?'

'Natalie, stay cool, it's me, Martin. Can we talk?'

'Not really.'

'Well, just listen to what I say then. Let's go out tonight. Let's go back to Dancemania, the rap club. Remember you first took me there, let's go for a laugh.'

'I'm sorry, I'm busy going to drama today and tomorrow I'm attending a dance class and an audition, so I really don't have any time.'

'Come on, Natalie, it'll be fun. I'll teach you some of those dance moves that you said you wanted to learn.'

'I'm afraid I must rush. I'm sorry I can't help you but I do wish you success.'

'Success,' he repeated, 'you wish me success.'

She put the phone receiver down and so did he. It was painful. He went to the bathroom, got back into the bath and soaked until the water went cold.

Later on that morning he found his father in the back garden replacing guttering. As his father worked away, Martin began to question him. 'Dad, when you met Mom, did you lust her or love her?'

His father stopped for a moment, raised his eyebrows as if he was searching into the distant past and declared, 'I did both, son, yeah, both at the same time.'

'Did you go out with her a lot before you got married, Dad?'

'No, son, we stayed in a lot when we were courting.'

His father seemed to be answering different questions from the ones he was asking but Martin continued.

'Dad, am I too young to fall in love?'

'Listen, son, ask your Mom, she knows a lot about that stuff.'

Martin realised that his dad wasn't in a philosophical mood. He shrugged his shoulders, scratched his head, and then went to see his mother who was watching television. 'Mom, I think Natalie hates me.'

'That's a bit strong,' his mother replied, patting the seat next to her where she wanted him to sit. 'She doesn't hate you. Why should she hate you?'

'Because she thinks she's beautiful and she wants beautiful friends around her and she never spends any time with me now. She's always doing drama or rehearsing or auditioning.'

'She's just trying to be an actress.'

'So, can't she be an actress with me?' Martin said, raising his voice slightly.

His mother took hold of his hand. 'Look, Martin, your friends are going to change, you know that. Even your girlfriends will change but whatever happens, your family won't change. We'll always be there for you. We love you come what may.'

'That's another thing, Mom. What's the difference between love and lust?'

His mother smiled and looked down into her lap, embarrassed. 'Well, Martin, love is when you want a person forever and lust is when you want a person for a bit . . . a bit of time that is.'

'So,' Martin said rubbing his chin, 'you can't lust someone and marry them.'

'You can,' his mother replied, 'but those marriages don't usually last very long. Love is the best, son.'

'Do you think Natalie loves me or lusts me?'

'I don't think Natalie knows herself, Martin,' she said, shrugging her shoulders.

Martin stood up and began to leave the room. 'I've got some thinking to do,' he said before heading upstairs to his bedroom.

There he made up his mind. He was going to the club tonight alone. He knew this was a bold move but he wanted his life back. He had a flashback to the accident. He re-lived his life being shattered but he told himself that his life was not going to stay that way. He was the captain, and he was going to celebrate. He began to search his wardrobe to see what he could wear. He pulled out his big blue Gucci trousers, his big blue Polo shirt and his brown Levi jacket.

'Mom,' he shouted downstairs.

'Yes, son,' came his mother's faint reply.

'I'm going out tonight, Mom.'

'Are you sure, son?'

'Yes, Mom. I'm going out on my own. I'll be all right.'

He laid his clothes out on the bed, positioned as if he was wearing them. Then he placed his underpants on top of his trousers and at the bottom he placed his West Ham football team socks. He looked at his old white trainers and decided that they were too worn out to wear. He had no choice, he had to wear his sensible school shoes. As he searched for his baseball cap, there was a knock, knock, knock, on his door.

'Who's that knocking on my door?' he asked. 'Identify yourself, parent.'

There was no reply.

'Who's there? Who's knock, knock, knocking?'

He opened the door to find no one there. He looked to the left and then to the right and found no one. Just as he was turning back into his room, dismissing it as an uncharacteristic joke, he looked down. There he saw the trainers he had nagged his parents for. A pair of trainers that cost £100. He picked them up and kissed them.

'Cor, thanks, Mom, thanks, Dad. They're brilliant, brilliant. These are the business, my dancing shoes, man.'

At nine thirty Martin was fully dressed and ready to go. As he looked in the mirror admiring his clothes, he remembered the last time he went to Dancemania and how he looked then. The more he did so, the more anxious he became. *Can I really do this?* he thought. Then the positive, honest voice of reason spoke to him. *You want to go, so let nothing stop you, just stay out of trouble. Don't accept any baddies from anyone and don't worry about people looking.* He jumped up and looked in the mirror again. *You're the captain. Celebrate.*

This time he spoke out loud. 'OK, number one, let's go for it.'

When he left the house he avoided his parents. He didn't want them to transfer their fears to him. Instead he shouted at the front door, 'I'm off, Mom, Dad. I won't be back too late. Bye. And thanks for the trainers, you're the best.'

At the door of Dancemania, Martin saw the two bouncers he had seen there before. He was now sure they were identical twins: they looked the same, dressed the same, and both gave him a friendly nod of the head. Once he was in the club, that sense of adventure he had had on his first visit returned. No one seemed to be concerned about Martin's face.

When he got to the dance floor there was room for nodding heads and bending knees only. The house was packed, with no gymnastics possible. The bass lines were even deeper than before. The frequency of the bass vibrated in the pit of his stomach. He hated the cramped conditions but he loved the music.

The place was so packed that as people moved around they would have to squeeze past others. On a couple of occasions people looked twice as they squeezed past Martin. But then a girl squeezed past and did not take her eyes off him. He felt very uncomfortable. He looked down but he could still feel her eyes on him. He moved to the music, turning away at the same time as he tried to cover his awkwardness. She turned with him.

He felt a tap on his shoulder and a voice shouted above the music. 'Martin, hey, Martin. Do you remember me? Marica, from the Jamaican sistas. How ya doing, guy?'

Martin glanced up. As soon as he allowed himself to look her in the face he recognised her. 'Yeah, I remember you. I'm OK. Yeah, I'm cool.'

'Where's Natalie and your friends?'

'They don't really like this scene, they're more into daytime activities. Mark's the leader of a new gang, they're called The White Knights. They spend most of their time hating everyone and trying to get excluded from school. What a gang name – he's got a lot to learn. Everyone makes mistakes but he should know better. He's missing all the fun. I see Matthew sometimes. Natalie wants to be a famous film star, she's on the telly.'

'So, you're on your own?'

'Yeah.'

'Come and see Teen and Naz. They're over there, in our corner.'

Over in their corner it was less crowded and there was more room to manoeuvre. The girls said that they really liked Natalie but they were surprised that they hadn't met her again. Teen handed Martin a half-full bottle of beer.

'No thanks,' Martin said. 'I'm trying to be a good boy.'

'So what, you still doing those bad dance moves?' she said jokingly.

'When I can,' he replied.

Naz joined in. 'After that night, everyone was talking about you. So are you gonna jump up and rock the house tonight?'

'No,' Martin replied smiling with embarrassment. 'I'm just taking it easy tonight.'

'We read about you in the *Echo*,' Marica said. 'It was bad news, man, but we know you're cool. So just stay cool, all right, brother?'

'Yeah, I'm all right,' Martin replied, now smiling like everyone else around him.

For the next hour they danced in their limited way in their little corner. In this better lit part of the club, many people recognised Martin from his last visit and he soon got used to the compliments that people were still paying him.

Just before he was ready to leave, one boy came up to him and said, 'I heard about what happened to you. Just stay strong – it's nice to see you here.'

When he told Marica, Teen and Naz he was leaving, they walked outside with him. All four danced as they walked. 'Hey, I heard you were a West Ham supporter,' Naz said as they got outside where they could hear themselves more easily.

'Yeah,' Martin replied.

'When was the last time you saw them play?'

'I haven't been to a match for ages but I've seen them on TV.'

'When there's a good match on, come with us. We go all the time, no one messes with us.'

'OK.'

'And don't forget, man,' Marica interrupted, 'we down here all the time, this is the place. The drug heads have been removed and those that dealt in violence have gone in silence. We the queens here, so come again and do some of those bad, funky, fitness moves on the dance floor. OK?'

'OK,' Martin said. 'Hey, is your school doing the gymnastics competition next week?'

They all shook their heads.

'What's going down?' Teen asked.

'Well, I'm the captain of my school team. We're in the competition next Saturday at Newham Leisure Centre. Come down and watch us,' he said, brimming with excitement.

'We may do that,' Marica replied, looking at the other two, who nodded in agreement.

Martin made his way home deeply inhaling the late night car fumes which were like fresh air after the stuffiness of the club.

CHAPTER 19

~ The Gang of One ~

That night Martin had a dream. He was the DJ in his own club. It was as if the accident had never happened. Martin was outside himself, watching himself. He had no scars or skin grafts. Natalie, Matthew, Mark and the Jamaican sistas were in the house and he was spinning the discs. There were hundreds dancing in the club but all the heat and smoke had gone. The people gathered in a circle around his turntables as if worshipping a new god. They bowed their heads and rocked their bodies to the beats he generated. When he shouted, '*Wave your hands in the air, wave them like you just don't care,*' they all waved their hands in the air. When he said, '*Jump to the rhythm,*' they all jumped to the rhythm. It was his party. Then he picked up the microphone and started rapping to a beat and the house went crazy. The crowd shouted, '*More, More, More.*' Martin surveyed his constituents, and he knew the grooves were good. Natalie came up to him and whispered in his ear, '*Martin, you are beautiful.*'

Martin, you are beautiful. Martin, you are beautiful. Martin, you are beautiful.

Martin woke up with the phrase still reverberating in his mind. He shook his head as if to rid himself of it but it stayed with him.

Martin, you are beautiful. Martin, you are beautiful.

For a moment he thought the whole thing could be a dream – the crash, everything. The morning sun was shining through the curtains. He slowly got out of bed. He couldn't feel his face. He walked over to the mirror half believing that he might find himself looking as he did before the dream, the crash or whatever might have happened. But it was not so. He wandered downstairs, poured himself a drink of water and went and sat quietly in the living room. Revisiting the club, and his dream, had brought Natalie back into his thoughts. *Maybe she's just confused and she needs time*, he thought. *But why did she wish me success? What does that mean? You don't need success to go to a club. Maybe she's trying to work out the difference between love and lust, maybe she really wants me but she's testing me out.* The voice in Martin's head drove him to the phone where, for the first time ever, he automatically dialled Natalie's number, without looking at his book.

'Hello, is Natalie there, please?'

'Who's calling?' It was Natalie's mother.

'It's her friend from the drama group.'

'Could you hold the line one minute, please, I'll see

173

if she's awake.'

A couple of minutes later, Natalie came on the line.

'Natalie, it's me, Martin.'

Natalie sounded half asleep and her tone was discouraging. 'Why are you ringing me so early? What's wrong?'

'Nothing's wrong. I just want you to know that I'm here waiting for you. Sort yourself out and then it will be like before.'

'Sort what out?' she asked, sounding a little more awake but puzzled.

'Just sort yourself out. You can be an actress, you can be successful. I can be a dancer, I can be successful. Doesn't mean that we can't be together. I dreamt about you last night. We were cool. Everyone thinks we suit each other. Those girls were asking for you at Dancemania last night. It was a great night, I missed you.'

'Stop it, Martin,' Natalie said abruptly. 'I want to be your friend but just stop taking everything so seriously. Things are changing, people move on.'

'Do you love me?'

'Martin, you don't even know what love is.'

'I know a lot. I know the difference between love and lust.'

'So, did you love Pat James?' Natalie asked with a hint of bitterness in her voice.

'Pat James. That was ages ago. And no, I didn't

love her, that was lust.'

'Why are you ringing me, Martin?'

'Because I still want to go out with you. I hardly see you anymore. What's up with you? If you don't like my face, just say so.'

There was a moment's silence. Then Natalie spoke. 'I'm going now. I'll see you in school. We'll talk then. But you must understand, things are different now. My parents are coming, I've got to go. Bye.'

The line went dead but Martin still kept the receiver to his ear for a few seconds. He got back into bed and lay without sleeping until his parents rose.

Once he'd had breakfast and a bath, Martin realised that his dream was just a dream. He was still not sure about Natalie but he chose to push thoughts of her to the back of his mind. The night at Dancemania, however, wasn't a dream. Memories of it cheered him up. He'd had a great night and he couldn't stop telling his parents about it. They were quite concerned.

His mother asked him, 'Is it safe, Martin?'

'Of course it's safe, Mom. Look how many of the other clubs have had to close down. Dancemania's been given the all clear.'

'I read the papers, Martin, those places are dangerous.'

'No, Mom, not there. Everyone's chilled out, I've never heard of any fighting there.'

'But how do they treat you, son?' his dad asked.

'They treat me like a homie.'

His dad raised his voice. 'I'll have no son of mine being treated like a homie.'

'What's the problem, Dad? A homie's just a home boy, a boy that lives at home. They just treat me like a home boy, from the hood. That's the neighbourhood, Dad.' Martin added cheekily.

'Well just remember, son, if you need a hand I'm here for you. You can never tell when those homies or hoodies are going to get out of hand.'

Martin laughed out loud. 'You two are crazy but I like having crazy parents.'

At lunch time Martin decided to go for a walk in Plashet Park. He walked around the park until he came to a small area where there were swings, climbing frames and roundabouts. One of the roundabouts was empty. He pushed it, jumped on and then sat on the floor of it. He looked up into the sky and watched the clouds as he spun beneath them. Then he closed his eyes. He was tired and for a moment he let his mind drift. The roundabout stopped but he kept his eyes shut until he was disturbed by whispers. He opened his eyes to find that he was surrounded by a group of about ten children, none of them older than eleven.

Some of the children jumped back and screamed. Others shouted abuse: *'Ugly man,' 'You're the bad man,'*

'*Dog face.*' The kids shouted to each other, '*Don't let him touch you, he'll kill you,*' '*If you look at him for long you'll go blind.*' Some of them picked up twigs and pieces of paper from the ground and threw them at him, shouting, '*Get away, bogey man,*' '*Here's you dinner,*' '*You haven't got no Mommy or Daddy.*'

There were so many of them. It was happening so quickly that Martin was speechless. He stood up and the kids backed off but they stayed close enough to carry on shouting their nasty words.

He shouted, 'Go away, will you,' but they got even more noisy and began to follow him. He turned around and ran towards them but they screamed louder and ran off in various directions before regrouping. He tried chasing them a second time and they scattered again. It was useless. *Which one shall I run after?* he thought. *What do I do once I catch one of them?* he thought. He gave up but the children didn't, they trailed behind him again.

Then he heard a woman's far off voice. 'Get away, you lot! What are you doing? Leave him alone!'

The children all turned around and ran off. Martin didn't look where they went, nor did he hang around to speak to the woman; he was too upset and he didn't want any pity. He just carried on walking home with his head hung low, depressed and disheartened. It was the worst he had felt for ages. After all that he had survived on the streets and at school, it took a group of ten year olds to send him to an all time low, he thought. He didn't know how to argue with a group of that age. He couldn't fight a group of that age. They seemed to hate him, they thought he was evil, they were purposely cruel. Their images and words stayed with him as he walked home. At the top of Plashet Grove he turned right and began to walk down the High Street. He felt as if everyone's eyes were on him. As Martin walked past East Ham station, he glanced in towards the ticket machines and photo booth. He was so shocked by what he saw that he froze for a moment. A shiver went through his whole body and he clenched his fist in anger. It was Natalie, leaning over the ticket turnstile, kissing a boy. Martin looked hard, making sure that he wasn't mistaken. But it was no mistake. It was Natalie. As he looked closer, he recognised the boy. His eyes were closed. Martin could see his face, which was leaning sidewards over Natalie's shoulder. It was the boy she was dancing with in the commercial. Then Martin remembered that they went to the same drama school, that they had been in the same commercial twice. It all fell into place. *He too has cute Mediterranean looks*, Martin thought. *He too has tanned silky skin and long, shiny bouncy hair.*

Martin walked home as slowly as he could and went to bed.

CHAPTER 20

~ Face Value ~

The next morning Martin woke up to the sound of his mother knocking on his door and calling him. 'Martin, get up. You'll be late for school.'

Martin put his head under the bedclothes and said nothing. 'Martin, can you hear me? Are you OK?' When she got no response she announced, 'I'm coming in.'

She looked around the room, which was unusually untidy. Martin's clothes, magazines and music cassettes looked as if they had just been thrown on the floor. His wardrobe door was open and his new trainers were lying at opposite ends of the room. She looked at the bed, seeing only the shape of Martin's curled up body under the quilt.

'Martin, it's time for school. What's the matter? Why didn't you eat your dinner yesterday?'

She stepped over the mess on the floor and sat at the end of the bed. 'Come on, Martin, you got to go to school. You're late. Your dad's gone to work. Your breakfast is on the table and you've probably missed assembly already.'

There was a muffled response from Martin. 'Leave me alone, Mom. I'm not going to school.'

'But you have to go, son. What's the problem?'

'I'm not going,' Martin said.

His mother stood up and walked to the door. 'I don't understand, Martin. You were beginning to like school so much. Why don't you tell me what's the matter? Maybe I can help.'

Martin didn't reply; he lay silent and still.

She closed the door and went downstairs, not at all sure what steps to take next.

Martin lay in bed all morning. His mother had decided to do nothing. She sat quietly downstairs listening for a sign of movement. At around eleven thirty she heard him go to the bathroom.

As soon as she heard him, she ran to the bottom of the stairs and called up, 'Martin, are you all right?'

'Yeah,' Martin replied in what was more like a grunt than a spoken word.

She then went to the kitchen and prepared him an egg on toast and freshly squeezed orange juice. She had hoped that he was starting to get up but as she entered the room carrying the food on a tray, she found Martin still curled up in bed.

'Martin,' she said despondently, 'here's your favourite, some egg on toast. I'll leave it on your dressing table.' She made room on the dressing table and left the food for him.

When she returned an hour later, the tray was still there. She could see that two bites had been taken out of one piece of toast and a small amount of orange juice had been drunk. She took the tray out of the room and returned downstairs.

It was a day of nothingness. She spent the day waiting for Martin to come to life and Martin spent the day waiting for the day to go away.

Martin's father arrived home at six o'clock to find his mother crying in the kitchen. She tearfully told him about Martin's refusal to go to school or get out of bed. He was convinced that something had happened to Martin at the club but Martin's mother wasn't so sure. She reminded him that on Sunday morning he had told them what a great time he had had.

'That gymnastics team, his music and going to the club have made him the happiest I've ever seen him, before or after the accident,' she said.

Martin's father ran upstairs with his mother following and burst into Martin's room. 'Right, son, I'm your father. You can talk to me. What's wrong, son?' he demanded.

Martin lay motionless under the quilt. His father paced up and down the room and his mother tried desperately to pick up Martin's clothes, magazines and tapes from the floor.

'Martin, it's your father here. If anyone has hurt you, you tell me. If it's something that you want, tell me what it is. We haven't got much money but you know we'd try our best for you. It don't matter what it is, we can sort it out.'

Martin mumbled from under the quilt, 'All I want is to be left alone. What's wrong with that?'

'You can't just lie in bed all day, lad. You have to do something. You have to eat. Life's hard but you gotta be a man about it.'

There was more silence.

'OK, son, you come down when you're ready. We ain't going nowhere.'

Martin stayed in bed, under the quilt, for the rest of the night, only getting up once to go to the bathroom. When his mother brought more food into his room, he didn't touch it. The next day was pretty much the same. He had very little breakfast and stayed in bed, missing school again. But he did choose to sit up in bed. It was as if he was in hospital again. He spoke slightly more but still very little. His father went to work as normal leaving his mother to do her best. At times when she was managing to get sentences out of him, she tried to ask him about this sudden downturn but Martin just shut up again. His father came home that evening and tried a softer approach, as advised by a work colleague, but that didn't get him anywhere either.

On Wednesday when his father had left for work, Martin put on his headphones and his pyjamas and began to pad around the house. His mother tried to persuade him to go to school but to no avail. She tried to get him to go for a walk but he wouldn't entertain the idea. Martin simply did not want to come into contact with anyone at all. He did not want to talk about Sunday afternoon to anyone and he did not feel the need for fresh air. He wanted to do nothing but hide away. At lunch time the phone rang as he was sitting on his bed doing nothing. When his mother answered the phone, he could tell that the call was about him. He went to the door, opened it very slightly and listened to his mother's side of the conversation.

'Hello . . . yes . . . this is Mrs Turner . . . oh yes, I was thinking of getting in touch with the school. You see he hasn't been well over the last few days . . . No, no he's not in hospital, he's here. He's just not well . . . Yes, he has talked a lot about the gymnastics team . . . Yes, I know he's the captain . . . Yes, I know it's this Saturday . . . Yes . . . Yes . . . '

There was a long silence as his mother listened. Like many other things, Martin had not given the gymnastics competition any consideration. Now he wanted to know what was being said.

She spoke again. 'Well, Mr Hewitt, if you hold the

line I'll just go and have a quick word with him.'

As she came upstairs, Martin ran into his room and sat on the bed. 'Martin, that's Mr Hewitt on the phone, he's a bit desperate. He said the competition's on Saturday and he needs to get the team together beforehand to do some last minute work. Will you speak to him?'

'No.'

'Oh Martin, you can't let the team down. And guess what, a photographer from the paper wants a photograph of you all together.'

Martin lost his temper and shouted angrily, 'No one's going to photograph me. Tell them all to piss off. Who the hell wants my face in the paper? I'm ugly. I'm a bogey man. I'm a bloody dog face,' and Martin burst into tears.

His mother was stunned by his outburst. She walked back down to the telephone not sure of what to say. 'Hello . . . Mr Hewitt . . . I don't think Martin will be there on Saturday . . . I don't know what to say to you. He just doesn't want to do anything anymore . . . No, I haven't spoken to anyone . . . I really don't know, it may have something to do with his operation, or the crash. He may be being bullied, I just don't know . . . Yes Mr Hewitt . . . OK . . . Thank you . . . Goodbye.'

His mother went into the living room. She was scared. She didn't know what to do. She thought that

184

trying to talk to Martin might upset him more. But she worried that if she didn't go and talk to him he might accuse her of not caring. Ten minutes later the phone rang again. Martin went back to his door and listened again.

'Hello, Mr Green . . . Yes that's right . . . I don't know. He's been fine, school and everything was going great, then he just changed. He went for a walk on Sunday afternoon and he hasn't been the same since. He hardly eats, he hardly talks, he doesn't do anything . . . Yes, that's right, it's this Saturday. He was really looking forward to it . . . '

There was a long silence, then . . .

'Well, I'll try, Mr Green. I can't promise anything and to be honest, I don't think he will – but I'll try . . . OK . . . About 11 o'clock. If not, we'll see you here at twelve . . . Thank you . . . Goodbye now.'

Martin began to try and work out what had been arranged between Alan Green and his mother. He could sense desperation in his mother's voice and although he was feeling depressed and downhearted, he didn't want to drag his mother down with him.

When his father came home that evening, he went straight into the living room. Martin tried hard to listen to the conversation his parents were having but the doors between them made it impossible for him to hear. He crept halfway down the stairs but he still couldn't hear anything, so he went back to his room, got into bed and put on his headphones.

Ten minutes later his father and mother entered the room. Martin turned off his personal stereo and his father went and stood at the end of his bed. His mother sat close to him on his bed.

'After I spoke to Mr Hewitt today Alan Green rang, the man from the hospital, the one you said you liked. He asked me to ask you to do something. Tomorrow he wants you to come in and see him. He said it need only be for a short time.'

'And what if I don't?' Martin replied as he dismantled his headphones between his fingers.

'He said he'll come here, but you don't have to see him at all if you don't want to. No one can force you, but you know that you can't go on like this. Just go and see what he has to say. He's had a lot of experience.'

'OK, OK, I'll go.' Martin sounded reluctant.

The next day Martin's father didn't go to work. His mother made Martin his favourite breakfast, which he didn't eat. He spent most of the morning tidying up his room and reconstructing his headphones. At ten thirty a taxi arrived to take them to the hospital. It was the first time Martin had been outside since Sunday.

When they arrived at the hospital, Martin's mind went back to his days as a patient. Smelling the antiseptic air and seeing those ceilings with their fluorescent lights was like meeting old friends. On reaching Alan Green's office, Martin's mother knocked on the door. Alan Green came out into the corridor and greeted them all.

'Hello, Mr Turner, Mrs Turner and Martin. I'm glad you could make it.'

The only major difference with Alan was that his ponytail had got longer. He still smiled a lot and he still looked like he borrowed his clothes from a rock star. Today it was black leather trousers, topped with a brown collarless shirt and a black leather waistcoat.

'If you don't mind,' he said looking towards Martin's parents, 'I'd like to see Martin alone first.'

Martin and Alan went into the office alone.

In the office Alan pulled two seats together so they were facing each other and they sat down. Alan flopped back into his seat as if he was at home relaxing and immediately began to speak.

'I'm really glad you were able to make it. I hope we trust each other well enough to allow me to get straight to the point.'

'Yes,' Martin nodded.

'Now, I know that you've been doing well. You decided to go straight back to school. Everyone says that you were getting on great. The whole school is talking about your gymnastics, then over the weekend you lost it. What happened, mate?'

Martin played with his fingers and stayed silent.

'I have to tell you, Martin my friend, whatever it is,

you can get over it. Life is going to do this to you, it will put hurdles in your way but you can get over them.' Alan paused 'Let me ask you a question. How do you feel about yourself?'

'I don't know. I used to feel OK,' he said, looking at his fingers.

'So what's changed?'

'I think people were just trying to be nice to me because they felt sorry for me but really small kids, they don't lie. They just tell the truth and now I know how people really see me and I don't like it and I don't like me.'

'OK,' Alan said as he began to make connections. 'What happened on Sunday?'

Slowly Martin began to tell him the story. He started from the good times on Saturday night and then he went on to describe what had happened in the park.

He ended by saying, 'I don't care about anything now, I don't care about gymnastics, school or anything. The only thing that's keeping me alive is my music.'

Alan had listened without interrupting. When Martin finished, he said, 'Look, Martin, we know that when adults or even teenagers react badly to you it has more to do with their problems and hang-ups. Children of that age are different. Some of their reactions come from their parents telling them that anyone with a face that is different from theirs is a horrible person. Some children on the other hand think that someone who looks different is someone to laugh at and insult. Some children even run from Father Christmas.'

'So what am I supposed to do in that situation?' Martin asked.

'I'm afraid there is no textbook way of dealing with kids of that age, they are too unpredictable. Sometimes saying anything just makes it worse. You must realise that this type of thing is likely to happen again. Don't be paranoid, just be aware. All you can do is learn how to cope with it. You done well.'

'There's something else I need to tell you. Something that's been getting me really down,' Martin said, thinking about Natalie and her actor friend.

'What is it?' Alan thought he had flushed Martin's problems out of him but it seemed there was more to come. But then Martin hesitated, considering the reality. *Friends will come and go, talking to Alan is not going to bring her back*, he thought.

Martin was stuck for something to say now that he had changed his mind. 'Sometimes I just feel angry.'

'So do I, mate. The world's not fair but if I hit people every time I got angry, my knuckles would hurt.'

Martin cracked his first smile for days. Alan continued.

'Martin, *we* also have a serious problem and only you can help to solve it.'

Martin looked surprised. 'What, me?'

'Yes, you. You see, Martin, there's this gymnastics team and they really need someone who's got the talent to captain them. They don't want no upstarts or novices, they only want the best. Do you think you can help them out?'

Even at this low period of his life Martin found Alan amusing. Martin still had a lot to think about, but after their conversation, he felt more prepared to face the future.

'I'll see what I can do,' he replied and he stood up. 'I really don't want to let the team down – we were doing some good work we were.'

Alan could see that this was a natural time to draw their talk to a close. 'Go for it.'

In the corridor Alan apologised to Martin's parents for taking so long and informed them, 'Martin can handle this. If he needs help he knows what to do.'

They were both surprised by Alan's confident tones but they could see that Martin looked much happier and more relaxed.

'I'm off to visit my family in Scotland this weekend but someone's standing in for me and I'll be back on Monday if you need me. Have a good weekend, Mr and Mrs Turner. And remember, Martin – they only want the best.'

Outside the reception area of the hospital Martin and his parents stood waiting for a taxi. Martin was trying hard not to listen to his parents heated conversation about hospital closures and the future of the welfare state, when he heard someone calling his name.

'Martin. What's up, man?'

It was Anthony, the boy Martin had met on the ward. Martin's mother and father were shocked by Anthony's disfigured face. His mother grabbed his father by his arm and pulled him to her.

'Anthony,' Martin replied. 'What you up to?'

'I had to come and see my doctor. I got another operation soon so they need to keep an eye on me.'

'How did you get here? Where's your parents?'

'My parents? I don't know, they've probably gone to some exhibition somewhere. That's all they do, go to art exhibitions. I came by bus.'

Again Martin was amazed by Anthony's self-confidence. He found it hard to believe that he travelled by bus, and wondered about the types of situations that he found himself in. *What would those children have done if they had come across him?* Martin thought.

'Who's your friend?' his mother asked.

'Oh, this is Anthony. Anthony – this is my Mom and Dad.'

Anthony reached out and shook their hands. 'Pleased to meet you Mr Martin and Mrs Martin. So,

Martin junior, how's Natalie?'

Martin's reply came without hesitation. 'I've finished with her, man.' Martin surprised himself. He hadn't realised he had made this decision until the words came out of his mouth.

His parents looked at each other with surprise.

'Well, I did say that she wasn't bad. That could also mean she's not good. You see, Martin, she may have been just too pretty. Now, don't get me wrong, I got nothing against pretty girls, some of my best friends are pretty girls, but sometimes they can get too big for their boots. I like girls that have had a few fights. My girlfriends have to have a few scars. It gives them a bit of character, if you know what I mean!'

There were laughs all round – even Martin's father thought Anthony was funny. His mother was pleasantly surprised.

'I wouldn't worry about her guy,' Anthony continued. 'There's plenty more fish in the sea – or dolphins in the ocean.'

'You're right, man – I'm moving on. She thinks she's the queen or something.'

'So now that you've been released from Newham Parkside on good behaviour, what are you up to?' Anthony asked.

Martin looked towards his parents before speaking. 'I'm the captain of my school gymnastics team. We got a friendly competition on Saturday at Newham

Leisure Centre. Come down and chill out.'

Surprised once more, his parents looked at each other and smiled.

'What, you gonna fly, guy?'

'Yeah, man. I got hip-hops in my flick-flacks and funky things in my Arab springs. I fly, guy.' They laughed and slapped hands.

A taxi pulled up and the family said goodbye to Anthony. Just before they drove off Martin's father offered Anthony a lift.

'No, it's OK, Mr Martin, I got my bus pass and I want to walk for a bit. I've heard that there are some dangerous, scar face girls around here!'

'See you Saturday,' Anthony shouted as the car drove off.

CHAPTER 21

~ No Great Loss ~

The next day after his father had left for work, Martin proposed a deal to his mother. 'I'll be a very, very good boy, I'll do lots of housework and I'll make you really proud of me if you let me stay home today.'

'I'm not sure, Martin,' his mother replied, 'every day at school counts.'

'But Mom,' Martin pleaded, 'it's the last day of the week. What I want to do is stroll into school on Monday morning victorious. My team, I mean our team, will be known as the champions. Let me stay with you, please, best mom in the world.'

His mother stepped towards him and held him in a long, warm hug. 'OK, but you'll have to earn your keep.'

In the event, Martin spent all of that day sitting in front of the television with his mother watching Australian soaps.

Martin knew that after school that day there was to

be a final training session. Watching the clock carefully, he let enough time pass so that most of the pupils would have left school and he then made his way to the session. Walking the streets again made him realise how much he disliked staying indoors but now he hadn't time for sight seeing or neighbourhood watching. He walked into the school playground and went straight to the gymnasium.

He entered to find the whole squad was gathered tightly around Mr Hewitt receiving words of wisdom. When they saw Martin, everyone had something to say.

'We thought you had gone to another team.' 'Aren't we good enough for you?' 'What are you doing tomorrow, mate?' 'Would you like to be our captain, mate?'

Mr Hewitt got right to the point. 'Right, we don't have much time. Warm up, Martin. We'll go through the exercises and when we've done the compulsory stuff, you can do your freestyle routine in your own time.'

The practice session was a good one. It didn't take Martin long to get back into the swing of things and it didn't take him long to realise how much he meant to the team. No one made any serious comments about the days he had missed. Everyone's concern was getting prepared for the next day. At the end of the session, Mr Hewitt gave all the team members brand new full leotards, sky blue with a large white **E** logo on the back.

'I had to fight hard for these. Look after them, they cost half of the school's annual budget!'

Just before they dispersed to the changing rooms, Martin felt a speech coming on. 'I've got something to say,' he announced. 'I'm sorry for missing this week's training and thanks for bearing with me.' The speech was a good idea but as soon as he started he was lost for words. 'Well, I just wanna say that tomorrow . . . we can do it, that's all I gotta say!'

Saturday morning was bright and crisp. The fields at the leisure centre had a light covering of mist on them but the packed gymnasium was hot. All the teams lined up whilst the Lady Mayor pronounced the games open. As Martin stood in line, he looked around for familiar faces. His parents sat with his school supporters but he couldn't see anyone else he knew. There were over four hundred spectators and he found that when he looked too hard, all the faces blended into each other. It was the first time for a long time that he had been in the company of so many people.

His heart raced, then he heard his name being shouted from amongst the crowd.

'Martin, look this way!'

He looked but couldn't see anyone.

'Martin, over here!'

He continued to look until his eye was caught by Marica and Teen wearing their *I love Jamaica* T-shirts. Next to them was Naz in a West Ham tracksuit. They were jumping up to get noticed and making joyful noises. In spite of his nervousness, he couldn't help laughing and he waved back.

Soon a voice boomed through the loud speaker system telling the crowd to settle down, and the games began. There were five judges, who had to judge the contestants on a rating of one to ten for each discipline. They were to assess each competitor's poise, balance, co-ordination, elegance, confidence in execution and correctness. At the end of the competition the points would be totalled.

The first competitors to compete were the trampolinists. There were two from each school team and Martin was one of those representing Eastmorelands. As he walked out to the trampoline, he became very conscious of his face. He knew that every person in the hall was looking at him. He was tempted to look around to see their expressions. Were they looking at a gymnast or a face? He was nervous but he tried not to show it. He would not give into temptation. He just stared straight ahead in order not to lose his concentration. He knew that this was a big test of his confidence.

When his name was announced, there was a roar of support for him. He could hear his mother encouraging him with shouts of, 'Go on, Martin, you can do it' and his father with, 'You're all right, son.' It all helped to calm him which in turn helped him to focus on his gymnastics. He was happy with his display which consisted of seat drops, knee drops, swivel hips and front drops, followed by a fine display of somersaults. He then watched other members of the team competing on the vaulting horse, the parallel bars, the rings and the asymmetric bars.

Then it was Martin's turn on the beam, where he did a series of balance exercises.

Just before Martin began his floor exercises, he heard a voice from behind him.

'Be cool and deadly, fly guy.'

He knew it was Anthony but he did not want to break his concentration, so he just looked straight ahead and began his routine. He took a couple of steps and did a turning jump. As he landed he did two hand springs and went into a front tucked somersault. He then did two cartwheels and an Arab spring followed by four perfect flick-flacks. As he reached the opposite corner of the mat and changed his direction, the crowd applauded. He did two head springs, a forward roll, and another Arab spring, followed by four more flick-flacks, ending on a superb back somersault, which commanded more applause from the crowd.

He saw the rest of the team punching the air with their fists and he knew he had done well.

As he walked back to the team's bench, he looked back to see Anthony. He was standing in the crowd being very loud. He pointed to Martin and shouted loudly, 'You see that man there? He is the man, he is the brother.' The Jamaican sistas shouted their approval and there were laughs throughout the gymnasium.

The main part of the competition was over. All that was left was the freestyle section.

Martin was certain that freestyle was his team's strongest point. The standard routines had to be executed according to rules laid down years ago but freestyle meant freedom. There were no precise rules to follow. All the judges needed to see was an inspired performance.

Eastmorelands were the last to perform which was the way Martin liked it. He watched the seven other schools do performances which were close to ballet, or performances with classical music. Then it was the turn of Eastmorelands. All eighteen members stood around the floor mat. First there was silence. Then it came. It was a mighty, hip-hop beat that shook the gym. Eight of the team, including Martin, took to the floor, dancing as they walked to the centre of the mat. When they got to a central point they simultaneously somersaulted backwards in time to the beat. They did some synchronised moonwalking before splitting off into pairs. Then came some fancy partner work: one partner threw the other under their legs, then over their shoulder. This was followed by cartwheels that took them out to the edge of the mat where the other eight, who had been hitchhiker dancing, took over. Martin and the other seven watched as their team members on the mat bodypopped like robots, hopped like Russian Cossack dancers and kicked the air like kung-fu fighters. Then Martin and the others joined them on the mat for the last section. The people in the house began to clap, their bodies swaying to the beat, and even above all the noise, Martin could still hear Anthony's comical commentary.

The performance finished with the team doing a series of somersaults around the edge of the floor mat. As they did so, Martin broke away and went to the centre. Finally the team pirouetted towards him, dropping at his feet into full splits on the beat of a big bass drum. The spectators loved it and leapt to their feet. Martin's parents stood proud, the Jamaican sistas were still dancing although the music had stopped and Anthony was informing everyone around him that he and Martin were good friends.

Through the loudspeaker a voice again demanded order and the spectators gradually quietened. All was silent as the five judges whispered to each other and wrote things down on the pieces of paper that they shuffled between them. None of the judges looked a day under fifty.

When the sports centre manager stepped into the centre of the gym carrying a microphone, everyone knew it was results time. He announced the marks given for each discipline and as he did so the scores appeared on digital displays above the spectators. Everyone struggled to calculate the overall winner.

Then the manager announced, 'Ladies and gentlemen, boys and girls. I want to take this opportunity to thank all eight schools for taking part in this competition and I am now pleased to announce the winners of the first Newham's Gymnastics Winter Friendlies. In third place we have Eastmorelands.'

There was applause from the fans and the team members embraced one another.

Mr Hewitt said, 'Well done, everyone, I'm proud of each one of you.'

Martin was a little disappointed but looked to the future. 'Yeah, well done – and we still got the freestyle winners to be announced, so watch this space.'

Martin's mother was clapping her hands frantically and shouting, 'Yes, yes!'

And his father was muttering, 'That's my boy, that's my boy.'

'In second place,' the manager announced, 'we have Saint Katherine's.'

The Saint Katherine's fans cheered and there was

more applause.

'And I am delighted to announce that in first place we have Compton Park.'

Compton Park fans cheered loudly and blew whistles, while the gymnasts hugged each other in celebration. It took a couple of minutes before the crowd settled down, then the manager continued. 'Now, as you know, we had a separate competition for freestyle.' The gym fell silent once more. 'And this special prize goes to the team that impressed the judges with the most original display of gymnastics.'

Eyes looked towards Martin. Martin was confident they would win this section: no other team had captured the audience as Eastmorelands had.

'This section has no runners-up, just one outright winner. But first, ladies and gentleman, boys and girls, I'm afraid that I have some bad news. Unfortunately Eastmorelands have been disqualified from this part of the competition.'

There was an almighty sigh that echoed through the gym. The shock waves were palpable. The manager continued, 'The judges have declared that their display was not appropriate, and that in their minds it was a performance of pop music dance and not a display of gymnastics.'

Martin raised his hands in disbelief, and the team members gasped. A disapproving roar came out from the crowd and the loudspeaker called for order.

'It gives me great pleasure to announce that the winner of the freestyle competition is Kirton High.'

Polite applause came from the spectators but Martin could not contain himself.

'They were crap,' he said, turning to his team mates. 'Listen to the people, everyone knows they were crap.'

Although Mr Hewitt sympathised with Martin, he felt that his language was a little too strong. 'Calm down, Martin, you may not like the judges' decision but that's no way to talk about your fellow competitors.'

'But, sir,' Martin fumed, 'we were the best, everyone knows that. We rocked the people, we got them moving. It's obvious that we were the most original.'

'You have to respect the judges' decision. I know you were good, you know you were good. Let's just say that you were a little bit ahead of your time.'

'Can't we do something, sir? Can't we make a complaint?' Martin shouted, as he threw his towel down on the ground. 'It ain't fair. Kirton High weren't that good, anyone could do what they done.'

Mr Hewitt picked up the towel and handed it to Martin. 'Calm down, Martin, no one's ever changed a judge's decision by complaining.'

'But we were the best, sir.'

'The best are not always the winners,' Mr Hewitt replied, touching Martin on his shoulder.

'Thank you for coming to our wonderful sports

centre,' the manager announced. 'We are open from nine to nine, seven days a week. And don't forget next year, when we will proudly present the second Newham Gymnastics Winter Friendlies. Goodbye, everyone.'

As soon as people began to disperse Martin began to talk to his team-mates. 'I'm sorry, it's my fault. Maybe I should have worked out something a bit more normal. I made us do all that work just to get disqualified.'

But his team-mates let him know that they were fully behind his ideas. One boy in the team said, 'We were the originals, we had it going – we wouldn't have done it any other way.'

Then the Jamaican sistas came down to see Martin. Marica tried to imitate some of Martin's dance moves.

'You should have won that, man. You should have won everything.'

'Yeah, yu bad,' said Naz.

Anthony appeared. 'Hey, man. I am pleased to announce that you are the winner of the business. Who's Kirton High? I saw better gymnastics in hospital.'

'Did you see what they done to us?' Martin said in reply. 'It's not fair, man.'

Martin's parents had also come down to see him. Although his father was unhappy with the judges' decision he was more surprised by Martin's new friends, who seemed to him to speak another language. He looked around in vain to see if he could see Matthew or Mark. The sistas and others in the gym tried not to stare at Anthony but most found they just couldn't help looking. Anthony by his very nature, by his loudness, not his face, was attracting lots of attention.

'Them judges need to be born again. They got no taste, they don't know quality and they got no rhythm,' said Anthony to Martin.

'You're the best, son,' his father said.

Martin looked at his mother, who simply added, 'You were great.'

Mr Hewitt produced bottles of mineral water from his sports bag and everyone drank it as if it were champagne.

'To our captain,' said Mr Hewitt, raising his bottle. 'And to our team,' he said, raising his bottle once more.

'And to all the funky dudes,' said Anthony.

Martin saw a group of girls leaving the gym. He recognised some of them as Natalie's friends from school. Then he saw Natalie walking towards him. He looked at her and then turned his back on her and spoke to those around him. 'Let's get out of here,' he said, picking up his bag and turning towards the athletes' exit.

Just then there was a shout. 'Mr Hewitt, oh Mr Hewitt! Any chance of that photo now?'

There was a moment of tension. The whole team knew Martin didn't want his photo taken. Everybody just looked at everyone else, then everyone looked at Martin. Mr Hewitt looked uncomfortable and sounded nervous. 'I'm sorry, I forgot to tell you, Martin. The *Echo* wanted a picture of the team. The team didn't want to do it without you, and I told the photographer that you're the boss.'

Martin looked at the photographer, then he looked back at Natalie, who was now standing still and watching. 'No problem,' he said.

'Right, we'll do it here,' said the photographer.

The team gathered together around Martin and the photographer began to click away. Martin's smile was at the centre of every flash and his parents loved it. As the last picture was being taken Martin pointed his finger at the photographer and said, 'Get a move on will you, I'm in a hurry. I can't just hang around modelling, you know. I've got to go to drama school today and tomorrow I'm dancing and making movies.'

Everybody laughed but none of them except Natalie knew what Martin really meant. Natalie got the message. She turned and walked away.

As the team, Martin's parents, the Jamaican sistas, and Anthony walked towards the exit, Anthony said to Martin, 'You should have won that. Don't you feel bad? Don't you feel cheated?'

'I feel cheated but deep down I don't feel bad.'

'I would, man,' Anthony said. 'I'd be angry. I'd be making loads of noise if I were you.'

'Well,' Martin replied, 'I feel sorry for my team but I don't feel sorry for myself.'

Then Martin stopped. He looked Anthony in the eye and said, 'It's not the winning that matters, or even the taking part. For me, it's the being here. Today I'm the winner.'

faceless

You have to look beyond the face
To see the person true,
Deep down within my inner space
I am the same as you;
I've counted since that fire burnt
The many lessons I have learnt.

You have to talk to me and not
The skin that holds me in,
I took the wisdom that I got
To make sure that I win;
I'm counting weaker folk than me
Who look but truly cannot see.

I've seen compassion from the blind
Who think with open eyes,
It's those that judge me quick you'll find
Are those that are unwise;
Why judge the face that I have on
Just value my opinion.

Friends will come and friends will go
Now I need friends that feel,
My friends have changed so much and so
I make sure they are real;
I took the ride and paid the price,
I can't afford to do that twice.

I came to here from ignorance
I cannot call it bliss,
And now I know the importance
Of loving me like this;
To leave behind that backward state
Of judging looks is very great.

I'm beautiful, I'm beautiful
This minor fact I know,
I tell you it's incredible
Near death has made me grow;
Look at me, smile, you are now seeing
A great thing called a human being.